Evelyn

My favourite Girl!
Tracie x

By: Tracie Podger

Copyright

Evelyn

ISBN- 13: 978-1500842475

ISBN- 10: 1500842478

About the Author

Hi, I'm Tracie and currently live in Kent, UK with my husband and a rather obnoxious cat called George. In between being a Padi Scuba Diving Instructor and having a full time job, I've managed to, so far, write four books with a fifth in the planning stages. I've been so fortunate to have dived some of the wonderful oceans of the world and it's only under the water, that I feel the most relaxed.

Thank you for giving your time to read my book and I hope you enjoy it as much as I loved writing it. If you would like to know more, please feel free to contact me.

Twitter, @Tracie Podger

Facebook, Tracie Podger, Author

or via www.TraciePodger.com

Out now

Fallen Angel

Fallen Angel II

Coming soon

Fallen Angel - Robert's Story

A Virtual Affair

Acknowledgements

I could never have written the Fallen Angel series without the support of my family. My husband has been my rock, without him, I wouldn't be here.

Huge thanks to a wonderful Author, Tom Ericson for all his help, encouragement and his involvement in the cover design, again.

My heartfelt thanks to the best readers and proofreaders a girl could want, Romy Lazzari, Janet Hughes and Paula Radell. Your input is invaluable.

I have to give thanks to the many people who bought Fallen Angel, Parts I & II and the wonderful reviews and messages I've received. I'm still humbled that you love what I do.

And last but certainly not least, a big hug to my publicist and friend, Paula Radell. She is one of the kindest people I've come across on this journey called self publishing. Paula is responsible for getting my books out there and I am overwhelmed by her support and belief in The Fallen Angel Series. Please see below for details of Paula's facebook page, take a look and follow. She is a huge supporter of indie authors and I am thrilled to have her on my team.

Paula Radell - www.facebook.com/curlupandread

So how did this all start? It's been a long journey but my love of writing came about after I was encouraged to do so as part of my recovery from depression. I have always loved to read and lose myself in books, words soothe me.

One day, after a series of dreams, I sat with my laptop and the words flowed from my fingertips - pages and pages of them. I forgot my troubles and lost myself in the characters I have created. I hope you can too.

There is no greater agony than bearing an untold story inside you - Maya Angelou

Contents

.

Chapter One

My day had gone from bad to worse. That morning I had taken my sister, Maria, to the doctors, again. She had always been a sickly child but since mom died she seemed to have retreated further and further into herself. My father struggled to cope so he immersed himself in his business. And the man I secretly loved had recently been killed.

****

I was sixteen years old when Rocco turned my world inside out, upside down. He had worked for my father, was his right hand man and although nearly ten years older than me, he had always shown me kindness. With his dark, wavy hair and hazel eyes, I would imagine him as a movie star, the subject of posters stuck on the bedroom walls of teenage girls. Instead, he ended up second in command in my father's business. And what business was that? The business of crime, the Mafia. For that's what we were, a powerful family in Washington, DC.

He had been sent to America from Naples by his mother and into the care of my family. I'd heard the rumours that surrounded him, He was ruthless, some said violent. People whispered about him, no one caught his eye and I felt a little sorry for him. He had been taken into our home, and I knew my mother was not happy about it.

Lying in bed one night I heard the raised voices from downstairs. I crept from my bed and sat at the top of the stairs to listen.

"He killed a man, Guiseppe," I heard my mother say.

"I know, but he did that to avenge his family," my father had replied.

They argued back and forth. I guessed my mother was not pleased that he had been given refuge in her home. My mother and us children had been sheltered from my father's business. We knew what he did of course. It was hard not to overhear the gossip, to see the house full of people, money, and, although my father never knew, I'd seen the guns hidden in the little shed at the back of the garden.

As I sat and listened, I watched the front door open, Rocco entered and the arguing stopped. I scrambled to my feet, trying not to be seen, but I had. He looked up the stairs and smiled at me. My face flushed before I quickly made my way back to my bedroom.

"Is he back?" Maria asked as I climbed into bed.

"Who?" I replied.

"Rocco, of course. I see the way you look at him."

"Go back to sleep, Maria, and mind your own business." I snapped.

Whenever I knew Rocco was in the room next to mine I couldn't sleep. I would toss and turn thinking of him. Of his hazel eyes and his soft voice. He didn't look like a killer; he looked just like any other normal guy, beautiful, but normal.

****

The following morning as I was helping mom prepare the breakfast, Rocco came and silently sat at the table. My mother gave him a forced smile but the tension was palpable, it sparked around the room and made me feel uneasy. I placed food on the table and as he reached forwards, his hand brushed against mine. I pulled back quickly, my face burning as I heard him softly chuckle.

"Go to the store, Evelyn," my mother said, as she handed me a list. Had she seen? Did she know how, at only sixteen, I was so affected by this man?

I rushed from the room, colliding with my father.

"Why the rush?" he asked.

"Papa, I'm sorry. I heading to the store, can I get you anything?"

I loved my father so much. He was big man with rough, calloused hands that would squeeze me tight to his chest as I sat on his lap. He would tell me stories of where he had been born, of the olive groves his parents had owned in a little village in Italy. He used to say that he would take me, always the next year, but we never went. My mother had told me that he had fallen out with his parents and my father, being the stubborn man that he was, would not forgive them.

As I entered the deli, the tinkle of the doorbell alerted the owner he had a customer. I was greeted with a hug, encouraged to sample a new cheese that had been flown in and to dip freshly made bread into warm olive oil. I handed over the list my mother had prepared and browsed, taking in the smells of the cheeses, the meats, the fresh tomatoes and listening to the chatter of the locals. Sometimes I would hear my father's name and the chattering would stop, people looking my way to see if I'd heard. But, mostly, I was welcomed and embraced.

Before heading home I would pop into the little watchmaker's and sit for a coffee with my father's oldest friend, Joseph. He was a kind man who always had time for me. He loved to talk, especially about the old days, the days when my father had first arrived. He would laugh at some of the mischief they got in to and no matter how many times I had heard the story, he told me how my father had helped him start his little business. I could recount the tale word for word, but I always sat in silence and listened. He wasn't an old man, but he'd had a hard life, making him seem so much older.

On arriving home, the house seemed empty. I stored the food away and started my chores. Curiosity got the better of me and I made my way upstairs. My hand rested on the door handle of the room Rocco slept in. I hesitated, listening before opening it. The bedroom was tidy with just a single bed against the wall, a dresser under the window and a cupboard for clothes. On top of the dresser I noticed a folded T-shirt. Picking it up, I raised it to my face, brushed the soft cotton against my cheek and breathed in the smell of him. And then I heard the floorboard creak. Spinning around I came face to face with Rocco wearing nothing but a towel around his waist. I stared at his stomach, the muscles still dripping with water from his shower and the tattoos that covered his chest and one arm.

"Oh, I'm sorry, I was looking for laundry. I was smelling, erm, you know, to see if it was clean," I mumbled, my face burning.

I couldn't look at him, staring only at his bare feet. He took a step towards me and I held my breath. He placed his fingers under my chin and lifted my head. His beautiful hazel eyes twinkled with amusement.

"Thank you, Evelyn. I took care of it myself," he said, his accent making my stomach quiver.

I could have died right then, from embarrassment. I amused him, that much was evident and I quickly pushed my way past and headed for my room. I sat on my bed and waited with bated breath until I heard him leave, the front door shut behind him. The sight of him, the smell of his clean, tattooed body filled my mind and I closed my

4

eyes. I felt a fluttering in my stomach that just wouldn't subside, and I fell in love.

****

I spent the next few months avoiding Rocco as much as possible. Sometimes it was hard, especially in the evenings when my father would expect us all to sit around the table for dinner. I couldn't look at him and if he spoke to me I would mumble my reply. I was the first to leave with the excuse of clearing the dishes or helping my mother.

One particular evening, the dishes washed, the table cleared, my mother and I sat with our coffees.

"He's no good for you, Evelyn," she said.

I looked up into her soft brown eyes, brimming with tears.

"I love your papa with all my heart, but this isn't a life I want for you," she said.

"I don't know what you mean," I replied.

"You do, my sweet girl. Be careful who you give your heart to, that one will break it. He is too old for you, too damaged already."

My mother met my father in Chicago; he had been in business with her family before deciding to move to Washington. The story went that she loved him from the first time they met. They were young and they struggled for a long time. Even after I was born, they lived in a one-bedroom apartment in a rundown block trying to juggle finances, prejudice and life. It was why the Italians stayed in one community where they could rely on each other for help. She was a young bride, with a baby, and far, far away from her parents.

She left me there to think, sneaking outside for her ritual evening cigarette that she thought no one knew about.

Only a few months later, just before my seventeenth birthday, my mother died of cancer. Thankfully it had taken her quickly, she hadn't suffered for too long. My father was destroyed, my sister refused to speak, and I was left caring for a toddler who would never know what a wonderful mother he'd had.

Chapter Two

My life changed the day I finished high school. I'd had plans for college but that was never to be. I had a family to care for. Joey was growing fast, Maria never left her bedroom, and my father relied on me to take care of the house. At night I would hear him cry, I would creep into his room and snuggle beside him. He would hold me tight and apologise for the life I now led. I was a mother, a housekeeper, a cook and somewhere at the bottom of the list, a daughter to a man struggling to cope. It was at this time that I began to learn just how powerful my father was.

People would come to the house, bringing gifts and food. They would be ushered into a room where my father sat. He was never without three men, Rocco, Jonathan and Mack. I knew my father owned a gym, I had visited a couple of times and would watch Mack box and sometimes, late at night, he would come to the house bloodied and bruised. Jonathan always looked so smart in his suit with shirt and tie. And then there was Rocco. Over the past year he had changed. He looked like he worked out a lot, his T-shirts would show off his broad shoulders, the muscles on his arms; and although he no longer lived at the house, he would always have a kind word for me. I still blushed every time I saw him, remembering that day in his bedroom. I still got that fluttering in my stomach when I saw him and I still avoided him whenever I could. My shyness crippled me whenever he was close.

My father conducted his business from home and I was growing uncomfortable with it. I was asked to make coffee and take it into his meetings, into a room full of men and cigar smoke. My father would be behind his desk and sometimes his guests would openly display their nerves; coffee cups would rattle in saucers. They often commented on how beautiful I was and fawn over me as if it would please my father, but one day a man took it a little too far.

I had made coffee and was placing the tray on a small wooden table in the centre of the room. I never made eye contact, nor would I speak, just deliver refreshments and leave. However, on this one particular day my father was entertaining a very well dressed man. He thanked me in a New York accent and as I turned to leave, I noticed his companion, standing a little away from the group. He leered at me as he placed an arm around my shoulders. I froze as Rocco leapt forward, grabbing the man by the scruff of his shirt. I watched in horror as he spun him around and smacked his head straight down on the desk. Blood spurted from his broken nose.

"Keep your fucking hands off her," he growled.

With shaking hands, I fled the room to the safety of the kitchen. I listened as the men left, the front door being closed and then my father came and sat at the table with me.

"Are you okay?" he asked.

"Who were those men?" I replied.

"Business associates, that's all."

"Papa, I know about your business, I know what you do. I have ears and I'm not blind."

"Evelyn, I care for my family, I provide, that's what I do."

"Please, papa, can you do that elsewhere? Think of Joey, of Maria. Move your business to an office, away from here." I pleaded.

He nodded and as he stood he pulled me to his chest. His strong arms wrapped around me and I felt ten years old again, comfortable in his embrace. I would never question my father for his chosen line of business but I didn't want it in the house anymore. I wanted the family to be separated from it.

"Why did Rocco hurt that man?" I asked as we pulled apart.

"He was just protecting you, that's good isn't it? No man will lay his hands on you, *bella.*"

I smiled up at him; his pet name for me, *bella*, meaning beautiful, always brought a smile to my face.

"Think about it, for me, papa."

He nodded and returned to his office. I started to prepare the evening meal, my back to the kitchen door when I heard footsteps come across the tiled floor.

"I'm sorry, you shouldn't have seen that," he said.

As usual, my stomach knotted at his voice, so soft, so very different to when he addressed anyone else.

"It's fine, Rocco." I said as I turned to face him.

"I've asked papa to move his business from here. There's Maria and Joey to think of, I want this to be a safe home for them. Perhaps you can talk to him?" I asked.

He nodded but didn't speak. We stood and looked at each other for what seemed like forever before he smiled, turned and left. For two years I had loved that man and I knew it was love. He was all I thought about when I woke and all I dreamed about when I slept. And yet, he was the one man I would never have. My mother had been right, he did break my heart, but he would never know that he had.

****

I woke the morning of my eighteenth birthday to Joey jumping up and down on my bed. He held in his little hands a stack of cards for me. As he snuggled under my arm we opened them. It was with shaking hands that I lifted the last one to my nose, I could still smell the faint hint of her perfume, sprayed over the purple envelope. It was a letter from my mother. Her flowing handwriting had written an instruction across the front. I was to open the letter on that day, not before. My father had come to sit on the end of the bed; he had kept this letter for me.

"Joey, come, leave your sister in peace," he called, making his way to the door.

Joey toddled after him and I placed the unopened letter on my bed. I needed time before I opened and read my mother's words. I showered and dressed, made my way to the kitchen with the envelope. I left it on the kitchen table as I sat with my family and opened their gifts. I was aware of my father's wealth and more so when I opened a beautifully wrapped necklace, a cross embedded with diamonds on a simple chain. Many years later I would see a similar version, worn around the neck of a remarkable woman. One I would come to love as if she were my daughter.

It was a wonderful morning. Joey helped to unwrap the gifts my father's associates had bought, although I was aware this was more to please him than me. Besides the necklace, the one I loved the most was a vintage Cartier watch from Joseph. I would take a walk later and thank him for it. Ushering them from the kitchen so I could clear the mess, I thought about the envelope. I wanted to be alone when I read the contents and I wanted to be close to my mother.

After retrieving my coat, I made my way to Joseph's. He had a customer but on seeing me enter his store he brushed him aside to pull me into a hug.

"Evelyn, happy birthday," he said.

"Thank you so much for my watch, I love it," I replied, showing him my wrist.

He attended to his customer while I made him a coffee in the little kitchenette out back. I heard the tinkle of the doorbell and joined him behind his counter.

"So grown up all ready, where has the time gone?" he said, kissing me on the cheek.

Laughing, I pulled the envelope from my bag.

"I have a letter from my mother, I thought I might take a walk to the cemetery and read it there."

"Such a beautiful woman, your mother. Such a shame, too. You're a lot like her, Evelyn. She had a kind nature," he replied.

We chatted for a little while before I gathered my things to leave. Kissing him on both cheeks I made my way to the church. It was a bright, sunny day and I was interrupted many times by people wanting to wish me a happy birthday. I thanked those that had sent a card, a gift, before finding myself standing at the steps of The Shrine of the Sacred Heart. Pushing open the door, I walked into the cool interior and a peacefulness came over me. I hadn't been to church in a long while and I wondered why. I didn't want to attend Mass but the calmness I felt made me miss the place. I stopped half way to genuflect, making the sign of the cross before placing my fingertips to my lips. I sat in the front pew, laced my fingers and bowed my head, resting my forehead on my hands. I prayed. For the first time in years, I prayed for my mother, my father, my family and for myself.

I prayed for the selfish person I felt I had become. I wanted for nothing, whether the money that bought those things was from crime or not, I only had to ask and I was given. We had food on the table every day and the best shoes on our feet and yet this church spent one day a week offering free haircuts to the poor, free food to the hungry. I decided that I would volunteer. I wanted to start to give something back to the community that so obviously provided my lifestyle, whether they wanted to or not. My father was not a bad man, he would lend money to those who needed it and he provided a safe play area for the children of the apartment blocks he owned. But I wasn't dumb; he would also put the fear of God into anyone who crossed him.

My prayers over, I made my way to the little cemetery behind. I knew my father paid for a grounds man to tend to the forgotten headstones, to the grassed areas, and he had paid for benches to be placed for people to sit and mourn. Finding my mother's grave, I ran my fingers over the words inscribed on the white, cool marble. I sat on the grass and with shaking hands I pulled the purple envelope from my bag. I stared at it for a while before gently sliding my finger under the flap and pulling out the letter.

My darling girl,

Today you become a woman and I am so sorry to have missed it. I wanted to live a long and healthy life, to be part of yours, to watch you grow, but it was not to be. It would be silly of me to ask you not to be sad, but find it in your heart to smile and remember the fun times we had. Like the time we had a water fight on that hot, summer day - your father was so mad at us! We were drenched and crying with laughter. Remember the day you held my hand when Joey came and your father was away? You were so strong, so grown up and you comforted me. Thank you for looking after my babies, although it is something I wish I could have done myself. As I write this, I picture your face, your beautiful brown eyes and long curly hair. You remind me of my mother, you have her kind nature. I would often come to your room when you slept, just to look at you, especially towards the end. I wanted to have the image of you sleeping so peacefully when I left you. I think you may have always known I was there; you would mumble in your sleep and reach out for me. I would take your hand and sing to you, waiting for you settle again.

My dream for you, my darling, is that you live your life, your way. You will fall in love and I can only hope your kind, wonderful heart is never broken. I know your father loves you very much and I can imagine that life has not been easy this past year. He cried when you were born. We were so very poor and he was working so many jobs to make the money we needed, to provide for you. But on the day you were born, he held you in his arms like you were the greatest treasure. You wrapped your tiny hand around his finger and he called you bella. And you were, my darling. You were the most beautiful thing I had laid eyes on. I didn't tell you enough how much I loved you, how much I treasured our time together, and I am so sorry for that.

You are a very special woman, Evelyn, and I will always love you. Don't mourn for me, don't sit by my grave and grieve for me, there is nothing there. I'll always be with you, a part of you. It's time to move on with your life, Evelyn, to reach for your dreams, achieve your goals whatever they may be. You would have given stability for the past year to Maria and Joey, now let someone else take some of that burden from your shoulders, take in a housekeeper. I know this because I know you, my darling. I know that you would have taken over the family, their care, but it's your time now. Start to live the life you've dreamt of.

Happy birthday, my bella.   Mamma xxx

I hadn't noticed I was crying until a salty tear landed on the paper I was holding in my hand, slightly smudging the words. I wiped it as best I could and folded the pages, placing them back in their envelope. I laid my head on the grassy mound of earth under my mother's headstone and closed my eyes, doing as she had asked, remembering.

****

For the rest of the day I was on autopilot. I made the evening meal, I bathed Joey and put him to bed; Maria never strayed from her room. I then sat with my father.

"Papa, I want to get a housekeeper in, someone to help with Joey and look after the house. I want to work, papa, to get a job."

"Evelyn, I don't know..."

I cut him off. "It's in my letter. Mamma doesn't want this for me and as much as I love looking after you all, I need to do something for myself."

He had no argument to that. We sat for a little while before he nodded his head.

"I'll start to look for someone tomorrow."

"I'm sorry. I left all this to you and it was wrong of me," he added.

Taking my book, I headed off to bed. Stripping off my clothes, I pulled a plain T-shirt over my head and climbed under the sheets. The day had been very emotional; it wasn't long before tiredness crept over me, and my eyelids closed. I was woken by a noise, the sound of someone bumping into a door.

"Shit," I heard.

I climbed out of bed and listened. I could hear someone in the bathroom. It wasn't my father and there was only one other man who had keys to the house. He cursed again and I heard a loud intake of breath as I gently opened my door and crept to the bathroom. I saw him at the sink, the cold water running over his hands, and I watched as he raised his head to face the mirror above. He saw my reflection; he didn't speak, just watched me. I took in the cut to his cheek and the splatters of blood on his neck as I walked towards him. The water ran red as he washed the blood from his hands. Silently I took a cloth, placed it under the cold water and raised it to his face, holding it over the wound. He turned to face me, his eyes closed as he sighed. He took a step forwards and rested his forehead against mine. One of his arms snaked around my waist and his hand gripped the back of my T-shirt. It was as if he was hanging on, needing me to support him. As he moved his hand up my back, he dragged the T-shirt with him. Moving his head, he found my neck and as he pulled me closer, his lips kissed just under my ear and across my jaw bone before they found mine.

I dropped the cloth I had been holding and placed both arms around his neck, my fingers gripping the hair at the nape. My heart was pounding as I opened my lips and welcomed his tongue. As his kiss got deeper, more urgent, he walked me backwards until I was pressed against the wall, his hard body crushed against mine. One hand held my face, his thumb running over my cheek as his tongue probed. I couldn't stop it, a small moan escaped my lips and this stilled him. He moved his head away and I watched a trickle of blood run down his cheek from the wound that had reopened.

"Fuck," he said before stepping away from me.

"Fuck, fuck, fuck."

He balled his fists and paced the bathroom.

"Rocco?" I whispered.

He held his hand up, as if to silence me and I was taken aback by this. I moved towards him but as I did, so he moved away. Perhaps he hadn't meant to kiss me, perhaps he hadn't liked it as much as I had. I was mortified that I had made a fool of myself. My first proper kiss and it had ended this way. I felt the tears prick at my eyes, the salty sting as they threatened to fall. I would not cry in front of him, I couldn't. I made to move back through the door but as I did, he raised his arm, blocking the way.

"Let me pass, Rocco," I said.

"Ev, I'm sorry. I shouldn't have done that. I am so sorry."

I swallowed the lump that had caused my throat to constrict and nodded. Ducking under his arm I fled to my room. I fell onto my bed and buried my face in the pillow. The tears that were so desperate to fall started to slide down my cheeks. I sobbed as quietly as I could. My chest hurt as the sobs erupted from me, the pain of the past year pouring out. I didn't hear the door open, I just felt the dip in the mattress as he sat beside me. He gathered me in his arms and I cried into his chest. His hand stroked my back, soothing me and he whispered words I couldn't quite make out, into my hair. Exhaustion took over and as much as I tried to fight it, sleep won.

****

I woke the following morning with a heavy heart and puffy eyes. I was totally confused by what had happened the previous evening. Rocco had kissed me like he meant it, like he wanted to rip that T-shirt from my body and I had wanted it just as much. But then he acted like he regretted it, but came to my room to comfort me. My head was spinning, my stomach was in knots, my lips were bruised and slightly swollen. I placed my fingers to them, feeling where he had been, trying to conjure up the taste, the smell of him. I climbed out of bed and headed to the bathroom before anyone rose. Stripping off my T-shirt I saw his bloodied hand print where he gripped it. I wondered where he had gone; had he left the house or decided to sleep in his old room? The room directly opposite where I now stood, naked. I shook my head to rid myself of the thought before stepping under the warm jets of the shower. The glass cubicle quickly misted as the steam rose, spilling out over the enclosure. I poured gel onto my hands, rubbed them together to create foam before running them over my stomach, my breasts and across my shoulders. I felt a tightening in my stomach, an ache between my legs. I squeezed my thighs together, while my nipples hardened under my touch. My breath quickened. I had done this before, especially over the past year when I'd woken, sweating and breathless from yet another dream of Rocco.

My hand gently smoothed over my stomach, through the damp tangle of hair until my fingers touched that place I wished his would. My swollen clitoris throbbed at my touch, sending little sparks of current through me, making my skin tingle. Goose bumps raced across my body causing me to shiver. My breath caught in my throat as the pressure inside me grew. Although I had masturbated before, I had never made myself come. I would always stop, feeling guilty and dirty, but not this time. This time I wanted to feel my body give in, I wanted to imagine it was his hands doing this to me, his fingers pinching my nipple, rubbing and teasing. I wanted him.

I was at the point of letting go when I turned my head slightly and caught sight of a figure inside the bathroom, watching me. I clamped both hands to my mouth to stifle my scream. I knew instantly who it was, I would recognise him anywhere. I made no attempt to cover myself, I didn't think he would be able to see through the misted screen but he would have known, by my movements, what I was doing. I let the water wash the soap from my body and then asked him to pass me a towel.

I opened the cubicle door slightly to reach for the fluffy white towel he held out. Taking it, I wrapped it tightly around my chest before stepping out. I wouldn't look embarrassed, I wouldn't look anywhere other than straight at him. As I walked past, he stopped me, he held my arm, the fingers of his other hand smoothing away a strand of dripping hair from my face.

"Soon," he whispered.

****

I kept myself busy for the next week, one day volunteering at the church. I was no hairdresser but I seemed to have made an improvement to one old gentleman whose hair was knotted from lack of care. At the end of a long day and while sweeping up, Father Carmelo handed me a cup of coffee.

"Sit, Evelyn, you must be exhausted," he said.

"Thank you, Father, it's been a long but enjoyable day."

"Your father is a very generous man. We wouldn't be able to do this, were it not for his donations. I wish we would see more of him though."

"I'll mention it to him, he seems to be so busy nowadays."

"Well, pass on my regards and now get yourself off home. I'll see you next week?"

"Of course, Father."

Placing my coffee cup on a table, I collected my coat and bag and headed off home. Our new housekeeper had started that week, someone recommended by Jonathan and I was pleased that it gave me the time to spend the day at the church. I hadn't seen Rocco at all. I'd asked after him, trying to sound casual and was told that he was away, on business. I didn't want to think about what kind of business.

****

"Go and see this man, Evelyn, he's looking for someone, for his office," my father announced one morning.

He pushed a piece of paper across the kitchen table with a name and address. A local company with offices I had walked past many times.

"You didn't ask him to take me on, did you papa?" I asked.

"No, no, he mentioned a job, I mentioned you, that's all."

I wasn't sure I believed him but I folded the paper and put it in my pocket anyway. I really wanted to work, to get out of the house and earn my own money. A little later in the day I found myself standing outside the offices of Richmond Inc. Pushing open the door I walked in to an empty reception area. A phone was ringing with no one to answer it, and the breeze I had caused when opening the door had made papers fall from the desk. I looked around, uncertain of where to go before picking up the papers and shuffling them into a pile.

"Can I help you?" I heard.

Turning, I found myself facing an older man with grey hair and with a harassed look about him.

"I'm Evelyn, my father, Guiseppe..." Before I could finish, he cut in.

"Ah, yes. Evelyn, come in, come in. Can you start now? As you can see, I appear to be very short staffed." He waved his arm at the empty desk, the phone still ringing.

"Well, I guess so, but what exactly do you want me to do?" I asked.

"You can get the phone for starters," he replied as he rushed off.

I lifted the receiver before I had even managed to find my way around the desk or remove my coat.

"Richmond Inc., how may I help?" I asked.

The caller wanted to speak to a Mr. Philips. I had no idea who Mr. Philips was. I explained that Mr. Philips was away from the office and asked if I could take a message. Replacing the handset I looked around. I found a pen, some paper and wrote the message down. And then I tidied the desk. From the layer of dust it was clear no one had sat here for a while. I found unopened post, some dating back weeks and it took me a good hour to sort the paperwork into date order. The gentleman I had met when

I first arrived rushed back into the reception area, slapping his forehead with his hand.

"Evelyn, I'm sorry, I forgot about you. Let me introduce myself and show you around."

Mr. Philips led me through a door into a hallway. He pointed out the restrooms, his office and the entrance to a large storeroom. All the while he explained that Richmond Inc. were importers, mainly foodstuff from Italy. He proudly announced that I had probably eaten in the many restaurants that he supplied. He wanted someone for general office duties, to answer the phone and deal with the mail. I could do that and so I settled back at my desk, pleased that I had my first job.

The day flew by and at five o'clock I covered the typewriter I had used and gathered my bag and coat. I made my way to Mr Philips office to let him know I was leaving. He was on his telephone but smiled and waved his hand. I set off for home with a spring in my step.

"Papa," I called out as I entered the house.

I heard voices coming from the kitchen and making my way through, I stopped, abruptly, in the doorway. Rocco had his back to me. I hadn't seen him in over a week, the memory of the last time burnt into my mind.

"Evelyn, come in, tell us about your day," my father said.

I shrugged off my coat and sat at the table. Rocco poured a cup of coffee and as he passed it to me, his hand brushed against mine. A spark of electricity shot through me, and my stomach clenched. As I sat opposite my father, recounting my day, I caught sight of him, studying me, out of the corner of my eye. He sat with his elbows on the table, fingers laced together with his chin resting on them while he watched me. I cursed myself for starting to blush.

"So, Jonathan has a girlfriend?' he asked my father.

This was news to me and I sat and listened to them chat, thankful that I could take the time to watch him instead of the other way round. I could have listened for hours to his voice, the lilt of his accent. I was mesmerised by his soft lips, watching the way they formed words, and was reminded of the ferocity of them when he had kissed me. Every now and again he would catch me staring at him and he would give me a small smile. My father seemed to be oblivious to the tension in the room, to the quick glances he would throw my way and I wondered what his reaction would be to know his daughter was in love. Would he be pleased to know it was Rocco that I was in love with? Somehow I knew the answer would be no.

Later that evening I sat in the garden room. This had been my mother's favourite room in the house, the reason they had moved here she had told me. One wall was glass and on a balmy evening it was nice to sit with the doors open and allow the smells of the garden to float in. I had curled up on the sofa and opened a book, wanting to get lost in the romance I was reading. I would substitute the name of the hero for Rocco and picture myself in his strong arms, being swept away to a beautiful destination, to be made love to and to live happily ever after. I was so engrossed in this fantasy that I hadn't heard my father call me.

"Evelyn, I have been calling you," he said.

"Sorry, papa, I was reading."

"I need to go away for a few days, business. Will you help me pack a bag?"

We headed upstairs while I sorted through his closet for suits, shirts and ties. My father always dressed well, even when we were very poor. I had looked through photographs of him and my mother, and no matter the quality of the clothes he was always smart. I packed a bag for him and helped him carry it to the door. Mack would always accompany my father and he was waiting by the car, the rear door already open. Paulo sat up front, in the passenger seat. I kept my distance from Paulo; there was something about him that made me very uneasy.

"Rocco will be here, Evelyn, call him if you need anything," he said as he cupped my face and gently kissed my cheek.

"I will papa, have a safe trip."

So Rocco was staying behind. I wondered why. If my father went away on business, normally he went too. A fluttering erupted in my stomach, my father hadn't said for how long he was going away but those words, '*soon*' echoed around my head. I returned to the garden room and to the fantasy that might become my reality.

****

The following day I decided to stop by my father's office after work. I had spent the day thinking of an excuse to see him. It came to me while walking to the deli to collect lunch and passing the movie theatre. I would ask for a ride to take me to see a film. It was quite normal for someone to drive me if I was to go out in the evening. During the day my father had no problems with me walking the neighbourhood but not at night. I would mention that I wanted to go somewhere and a car would be ready and waiting, outside the house.

The door to my father's office was nestled between a deli and a pizzeria, both of which he had interests in. I pushed open the door and entered the dingy stairwell letting my eyes adjust to the low light before climbing the stairs. At the top I nodded to Ricardo, sitting in a broken armchair, a cigarette dangling from his lips. Pausing, I heard raised voices, a man and a woman arguing. I sucked in a breath and walked into my father's office. The sight that greeted me, knocked the breath from my lungs. Rocco was holding a woman to his chest, stroking her hair, comforting and murmuring to her. Her arms were around his waist, her hands clenching his shirt. She raised her head, her eyes met mine and she took a slight step back causing Rocco to turn his head, to follow her gaze.

"I'm, erm, I'm sorry, I'll come back later," I stammered.

As I backed out I heard her speak, not in Italian but her own regional dialect. I couldn't understand all of what she said, but got enough to know that she was asking who I was. I rushed down the stairs, through the door and quickly walked to the end of the block. I rounded the corner and rested my back against the wall, breathing in deep and slow to calm myself. I closed my eyes and saw the image of them together, it caused tears to form in my eyes and I angrily brushed them away.

"Bastard," I whispered.

"Who, me?" I heard and opened my eyes.

"She's my sister, Evelyn. You ran before I could introduce you," Rocco said.

"Oh, I..." I didn't finish the sentence as he closed the gap between us.

His hands snaked around my neck, his fingers pushing my chin up. His face was so close I could feel his breath, smell the faint hint of cigarettes mixed with his musky aftershave as his lips just gently brushed against mine. I raised my arms, around his neck, my hand on the back of his head pushing him closer but the interruption of laughter made him pull back. He smiled as his fingers trailed down my cheek.

"What did you want to see me for?" he asked.

I let my arms fall to my side, a sigh escaped the lips I so desperately wanted him to kiss and he took a step back, placing a respectable distance between us.

"I wanted to see a movie tonight, I need a car."

"Who are you going with?"

"No one, I just want to do something this evening."

"You can't go to the movies alone, Evelyn," he replied.

"I can, I don't exactly have a list of friends to invite, do I?"

I didn't have any friends. There were people I had known in school that I would stop and chat with, but for a while I had concentrated on looking after the family, I didn't have time to socialise, to go to parties. And I was never invited, the one downside to having the father I had. The parents of my school friends would never invite me for a sleep over, for dinner after school, in fact, most discouraged their children from being too friendly, period.

"How about dinner?" Rocco asked.

"Dinner?"

"Yes, you know that thing we do in the evenings. I'll pick you up at seven," he said, with a chuckle.

"Okay, that would be lovely."

With just a brief kiss to my cheeks, Rocco made his way back to the office and I was left stunned by the thought of my first dinner date. Looking at my watch, I noticed the time. It was already late afternoon and I made my way back home. The housekeeper was feeding Joey, so I headed for the shower. After, with just a towel wrapped around me, I scanned the clothes in my closet. Rocco hadn't mentioned where we would dine and I was unsure of what to wear. It was to be my first real date. I selected a white summer dress with big red poppies that would show off my tanned shoulders and arms. It was nipped in at the waist but flared out slightly to my knees. My mother had always commented that I looked like a fifties pin-up when I had worn it previously. It suited my figure. I wasn't slim, neither was I overweight but I had that hourglass shape that suited the dress. I sat and dried my long chestnut hair, curling the ends, and applied some makeup. I wasn't an expert at doing my own makeup, years ago Maria and I would practice, but she was far better than me.

Just before seven I popped my head into Maria's room.

"I'm going out, you will keep an eye on Joey, won't you?" I said.

"Where are you going?" she asked.

"Just out with a friend."

With that she returned to her book. I worried about her and had previously spoken to my father. I had wanted the doctor to see her. She hardly left her room, preferring to sit with her books, lost in her fantasies. I guessed it was her way of grieving but as time had gone on, we seem to have lost her as she retreated further and further into her own little world. I knew I could rely on her to keep an ear open for Joey though, although it was unlikely he would wake until the morning.

I headed downstairs with ten minutes to spare and sat at the kitchen table, the heart of the house. As each minute ticked by my heart rate increased, my palms became sweaty and I was conscious not to rub them over my dress. I heard the key in the front door, it opened and I stood. He walked into the kitchen and I drank in the sight of him. He was wearing a plain white shirt, open at the collar and I could see the faint black of his tattoos through the material.

"You look beautiful, Evelyn," he said as I gathered my bag.

"Thank you," was all I managed before lowering my head to conceal the blush I knew had crept up my neck.

He chuckled, "Come on, we don't want to be late."

Following him to the door, he opened it, stepped aside and with his hand on the small of my back, he ushered me to the car. He opened the car door and waited until I had settled in my seat before making his way around to the driver's side. He had learnt well. My father had many *rules* and one was that the passenger side of the car was always next to the sidewalk. "Never let your passenger have to walk into the traffic," he would say.

Rocco started the car and pulled away; he fiddled with a packet of cigarettes, shaking one loose before winding down his window slightly.

"Do you mind?" he gestured with his lighter.

"No, of course not," I replied. "Where are we going?"

"A little place I know, quiet, but you'll like it. They have the best veal."

We settled into a comfortable silence and without it being too obvious, I watched him concentrate on the road, on smoking his cigarette, on his lips as he inhaled. He cursed in Italian as the car in front braked sharply and he placed his arm across my chest to stop me being thrown forwards as he, too, braked hard. The touch of his hand on my skin sent shock waves through me and left a tingling when he removed it. It wasn't long after that he pulled up outside a small bistro. Opening the car door for me, he took my hand and led me into the restaurant. He was immediately greeted by the owner, ushered to a table towards the back and fussed over. Menus were placed on the table with a wine list and jug of water. Breads were left in the centre with a small bowl of oil. I watched him tear a piece of bread and dip it into the oil before placing it in his mouth, the oil leaving a glisten on his lips before his tongue swiped across them.

"Here, taste," he said, tearing off another chunk.

I shivered when his fingers touched my lips as he placed the bread in my mouth.

"The oil is from my family's farm," he said.

"Tell me about them?" I asked.

He lent back in his chair and I saw a flash of anguish cross his face. I leant forwards and took his hand in mine.

"You don't have to," I said, gently.

"My father was murdered, Evelyn, my brother too. They came in the night, dragged them from the house in front of my mother, my sister and me. I watched as they were taken away, I never saw them again. I will never forget my mother's screams as she tried to wrestle with them, before they threw her to the ground."

His voice was angry, the hurt very evident in his eyes as he stared at me. We were interrupted by a waiter placing a carafe of red wine and two glasses on the table. He stood back with his pad and pen poised, waiting to take our order.

"Five minutes," Rocco said, angrily.

The waiter scuttled off. I rubbed my thumb over his knuckles and I watched as he started to relax again. His shoulders slumped a little and he gave me a small smile.

"I waited ten years and then I got my revenge."

"And then you came here?" I asked.

"Yes, your father knew mine, my mother sent me here to protect me, to make sure I was safe."

"I'm glad she did," I replied.

We fell silent for a moment while we scanned the menu and on closing them, the waiter made his return. Orders placed, I sipped the wine that had been poured. An earthy, fruity taste hit my senses as I savoured the flavour. We chatted back and forth. He asked me about my work, he knew Mr Philips, about my hobbies, I had none and we laughed at childhood experiences we shared. He was easy to talk to; the conversation flowed with the only break coming when our food arrived.

I was very aware, however, of the tension from the staff when they approached him. It was the same feeling I picked up on when people were around my father. There was a hesitation, a need to please and I knew then, his position in my father's business was an important one.

"Is your sister okay?" I asked as we sipped our coffee.

"She came to tell me that there is trouble at home. My uncle runs the farm now and she wants me to return."

My breath caught in my throat at the thought of him leaving and then a feeling of guilt that I wanted to keep him here and not let him help his family.

"What will you do?" I asked, my voice shaking slightly.

"I can't go back, not yet. I'll try to sort it from here."

I was relieved, "Papa will help, won't he?"

"Probably, I'll speak with him when he returns. And talking of your father, I don't think he would be pleased to know you were here, with me."

I hadn't thought once about what my father would think. I would only hope that he would be happy for me. Yes, Rocco was older than me in years but mentally I had grown so much in the past year, I didn't feel my age. But, did he have a point? My father's upset was a risk I was willing to take. If he could see how much I loved Rocco he would have to give his blessing. But then, I had no idea how Rocco felt about me and it wasn't a question I was about to ask. However, the thought that my father might disapprove spoilt the mood somewhat. We finished our coffee in silence. Rocco took his wallet from his trouser pocket, peeled off some bills and held out his hand as he stood. I let his warm hand cover mine as he led me from the restaurant. Instead of heading for the car, we walked a block to a small park area. Rocco led me to a bench, in front of a pond and we sat under the glow of a street lamp. He placed his arm around my shoulder and I leant into his side, comfortable in his embrace.

"Thank you for tonight," I said. "I've really enjoyed myself."

"It was a pleasure, Evelyn. It's nice to be able to relax and enjoy myself as well."

His fingers ran across the top of my shoulder, slightly brushing the strap of my dress to one side. He turned towards me and with his other hand he stroked his fingers down my cheek.

"You are so beautiful," he said, gently.

His thumb ran across my lower lip and I parted them slightly, the tip of my tongue just catching the pad. I wanted to give myself to this man, I wanted him to take me there and then, to feel him inside me, to have him make love to me. I wanted to rake my nails down his muscular back and look into his eyes as he fucked me. I blinked, rapidly, to clear the thoughts, I took a deep breath to calm my nerves. I raised my hand to his cheek and he leant slightly into it. I could feel the roughness of the stubble around his jaw scratch my palm and I could feel a pulse beat frantically in his neck.

His kiss was deep and wanting, his teeth nipped at my lips, at my tongue as his hand fisted in my hair, pulling my head towards him. My hands gripped the front of his shirt and his moan reverberated through me. I felt like I was going to combust, a heat crept over me as dirty thoughts flooded my mind. I pictured him lying naked on top of me, his hard body pressing mine deep into the bed. I pictured kissing his stomach, those tattoos, as his fingers, his tongue roamed my body. A slight breeze had picked up and I shivered.

He pulled away, his hand found mine and as he stood he pulled me to my feet. To say I was disappointed was an understatement, I hadn't wanted that kiss to stop. My tongue ran across my lower lip savouring that last taste of him. He pulled me to his chest, his arms around me and kissed the top of my head.

"I need to get you home, Evelyn, it's getting late," he said, softly.

"I don't have a curfew, Rocco," I protested.

29

"No, but if we stay here any longer, I'm going to do something we both might regret."

He might as well have just stabbed me in the heart. I closed my eyes and let my forehead fall to his chest. Why would he regret this? I moved away from him, pulled my hand free of his and turned to walk back the way we came. He didn't follow me immediately but it wasn't long before I heard his footsteps. I arrived back at the car and waited for him to unlock the door, open it and I climbed in without looking at him. We drove the short distance home without speaking. As the car pulled to a stop I reached for the door handle. I felt his hand on my thigh and I stilled.

"Wait, you misunderstand me," he said.

"What do I misunderstand, Rocco? You kiss me like you mean it. You tell me 'soon' and leave me for days on end. You play me like I have no feelings," I replied, my voice rising in anger.

"Oh, I mean it, Evelyn. Every second your mouth is mine don't you think I want more, don't you think I want to throw you down and take you there and then? I want your body, I want every inch of you. I want to taste you, to fuck you. I want to own you. I want to be your first."

"Then why don't you," I whispered.

"Because your father would kill me."

I pushed open the car door so violently it sprang back and caught my leg as I exited. I cried as I scrambled out and limped as quickly as I could to the front door. I had my keys in my still shaking hands and I fumbled with the lock. I felt him behind me, he reached over and took the key from me, placed it in the lock and opened the door. I wouldn't turn as I pushed my way into the house, forcing the front door closed behind me, shutting him out. I leant my back against it and slid down, sitting on the cool tiled floor letting tears fall down my cheeks. I was in love with a man scared of my father's reaction and I cursed him. I cursed my father for being who he was, for the realisation that no matter what man I fell in love with, there would always be this gigantic barrier that was Guiseppe Morietti.

Kicking off my shoes I headed to the kitchen, I knew Rocco hadn't left, I could hear the car still idling outside. I needed ice and finding some, I wrapped the cubes in a cloth before sitting and placing it on the obvious bruising to my leg. It was dark and I just sat and listened to the ticking of a clock trying to slow my racing heart. Was my life always to be this way? How would I ever meet, marry someone if my father was always going to be an obstacle? I loved my papa but right at that moment, I wished I was just a normal girl from a normal family. I so desperately wanted my mom.

I heard the creak of a floorboard above and the gentle steps of someone creeping down the stairs. I wiped away my tears and planted a smile on my face as Maria entered the kitchen. She surprised me by coming to my side and pulling me into a hug.

"I saw you from the window, I wasn't listening but you looked upset," she said.

She was two years younger than me and she held me while I cried again, like I wished my mother could.

"I won't tell anyone, you deserve a life, Ev," she said.

"He doesn't want me, he's too scared of papa."

"You'll find a way, I know you will. I've seen the way he looks at you, I know he wants you."

I giggled, she giggled and before we knew it we were both laughing, covering our mouths so as not to wake the housekeeper or Joey.

"Did you kiss him?" she asked.

I nodded.

"Well, what was it like?"

"Oh, Maria, like savouring your favourite ice cream, but hot," I said before we both collapsed with laughter again.

I looked at her and it dawned on me, I hadn't heard her laugh for over a year, I hadn't seen her smile for so long. I smoothed her hair from her face and hugged her to me. I kissed the top of her head and hand in hand we climbed the stairs and headed to our rooms and to bed. I slid off the dress and kicked it to the corner. Sadness engulfed me as I climbed under the covers with just the glow of the moon lighting the room. Sleep wouldn't come easily, my mind full of thoughts and memories of my evening. My lips tingled when I thought of him kissing me and my stomach quivered. I curled in a ball, not allowing myself to feel aroused by those thoughts as I willed myself to sleep.

****

I woke early, the sun still rising over the horizon and I decided I would go to Mass. I wanted the serenity of the church to calm me. I dressed and headed out. I sat at the back and listened to Padre Carmelo, his voice soothing the jumble of thoughts in my head. At this early hour, the church was only half full and I felt myself start to relax. Just before the end I left my seat and quietly made my way to the door. It was then that I saw him, standing in the shadow, watching me. Had he followed me? He reached for my hand and pulled me into an alcove, out of sight.

"Here for forgiveness?" I spat at him.

"Yes," Rocco replied.

"For what we've done?" I asked, hurt.

"No, for what I'm about to do."

He grabbed my hand and pulled me to the door. The sunlight blinded me momentarily as we made our way down the steps and to his car. Silently, he opened the door and guided me a little roughly, in. He drove, fast, to the house he was living in, one my father owned. Taking his key, he opened the front door and pulled me inside.

Before the door had closed he took my hands in his, backing me to the wall as his lips found mine. He raised my hands above my head, his body pinning me as his mouth devoured mine. I could hear myself pant, I could hear myself moan and I felt no shame. I wanted him. I wanted him so badly it hurt. His kiss was deep, claiming, his tongue tangling with mine. His teeth pulled at my lips, bruising them and his hands clenched, holding on to me tightly.

When he pulled away, I couldn't catch my breath, my chest was heaving, my heart pounding so hard. He took my hand and led me up the stairs. The closer to his bedroom we got, the more nervous I began to feel, butterflies danced and fluttered in my stomach. He opened his door and led me into a large room. His bed was unmade as if he had rushed from it not so long ago, the previous nights clothes were thrown over a chair in the corner and the blind was still down. I stood in the middle of the room, shaking with nerves.

"Your sister?" I said.

"She's staying with a cousin," he replied as he stepped towards me.

With both hands, he unbuttoned the cardigan I was wearing and slid it from my shoulders. He reached around and found the zip of my dress which he slowly lowered. It fell, pooling around my feet. I crossed my arms over my chest, self-conscious. He peeled them away, holding them to my side as he looked at me. I could feel the heat in my cheeks as I blushed. He stepped back and pulled his shirt over his head, kicked off his sneakers leaving him barefoot with his jeans hanging on his hips. Taking my hands, he placed them on his chest. My fingers traced the many tattoos, my hands felt the muscles that twitched under my touch. I watched him close his eyes as I explored his body and he held his breath as my hands moved to the top of his jeans. I undid the button, the zipper and watched as they fell.

Oh, God. His erection sprang free, he was naked under his jeans and I couldn't stop my hand reaching down, desperate to feel the silkiness, the hardness of him. My hand enclosed around him, I felt him twitch as I slid it up and down, my thumb brushing over the tip of his hard cock. It was as if I instinctively knew what to do. He raised his hand to the back of my neck, his fingers twisting in my hair as he pulled me towards him.

"You can stop this anytime you want, just say the word, Evelyn," he whispered.

I released my grip on him and reached behind to unclip my bra, I wanted this, so much. I had wanted this for a long time. I slid off my panties and stood, letting his eyes wander over my body. He held my face, his mouth so close to mine, I could feel his breath on my lips. He walked me backwards until I hit the side of his bed. With one arm he held me as I lowered, the other stopping himself from falling on me, all the time his mouth did not leave mine. With a nervous giggle I scooted up the bed. Lying on my back I watched him as he crawled up my body, his arms holding him above me. He kissed my neck, across my collarbone and slowly made his way down my chest. His mouth found a nipple and he gently licked, nipped and sucked. My hands fisted in his hair and I pushed my body up, forcing myself further into his mouth.

The feelings inside my body were divine and I moaned out loud. His fingers caressed one nipple, his mouth the other. My skin felt on fire under his touch, my body shivered with desire and a heat raged between my parted legs. I guess he felt he had given my nipples enough attention because his lips moved to my stomach, little kisses as he made his way down my body. His tongue flicked in and out of my navel and then further down to the top of my thigh. Oh, God, he was going to kiss me, there. I tensed, my hands fisted in the sheets we were lying on. I could feel his cool breath against my heat and I screwed my eyes shut, tightly.

"Relax," he whispered.

On his command, I released the grip on the sheets, my body relaxed back into the bed and I just let those new sensations wash over me. With his hands, Rocco held the inside of my thighs and parted my legs further, exposing myself to him. His nose ran over my clitoris, his thumbs gently parted me and when his tongue licked its way over my opening I cried out. I heard a soft chuckle as his tongue probed. Something happened inside me, an explosion of sensation, uncontrollable waves of, well, I'm not quite sure, rolled over me. My body arched off the bed and as it did so the pressure of his thumb on my clitoris, the probing of his tongue intensified. I cried out again, my breathing sped up and all I craved was release of a pressure building up inside me. And when it came so did the tears. Big fat droplets of salty liquid squeezed from my eyes, rolling down the sides of my face as I gave in to my orgasm. I felt him crawl back up my body, his lips sealed over mine and I tasted a tangy, metallic taste on them. I tasted me. My arms gripped around his body, my fingers dug into his back as the tip of his cock brushed against my opening.

"Are you sure?" he asked. I could only nod my head.

He reached over to his nightstand, opened the drawer and pulled out a condom. Ripping open the packet with his teeth, he rolled it down his cock. Holding my hands above my head, he very gently pushed himself inside me. It burnt, it stretched me and just when I relaxed my stomach muscles, he thrust into me then stilled. I bit down on my lip to stifle the scream against a sharp bite of pain which quickly subsided.

"Okay?" he whispered. Again, I could only nod my head.

He moved so gently, so smoothly and the more I relaxed the more I wanted him, faster, harder. I wrapped my legs around his waist, forcing him deeper and I rocked my hips towards him, in time with his movements. His head was nestled in my neck, he whispered words and he fucked me. I loved every second of it.

I felt his body tense, the grip on my hands tighten. He moaned, he called out my name as his body shuddered. He stilled not wanting to pull out of me. Lifting his head, he smiled. I couldn't help but laugh, I felt euphoric.

"This is going to sting," he said as he eased himself out of me.

I winced slightly as he rolled to one side, pulled off the condom and dropped it to the floor. I turned on my side to face him, he pulled me to his chest as he dug beneath us to pull the sheet around our sweaty bodies.

"How do you feel?" he gently asked.

"Wonderful, sore," I laughed.

He chuckled as he nestled me against him. My head rested on his shoulder, my arm over his chest. I listened to his heart beating and a wave of tiredness came over me. I closed my eyes and drifted off.

****

I was woken by a finger trailing up and down my side, goose bumps followed his touch. I slowly opened my eyes and raised my head to look at him. His smile dazzled me, the tenderness in his look overwhelmed me and tears pricked at my eyes again.

"Hey, don't cry, it wasn't that bad, was it?" he joked.

"No, I don't know why I'm crying," I laughed.

"Come on, let me run you a bath. It'll help."

I found out what he meant when I tried to sit up and climb from the bed. I felt very sore and a wetness between my legs. I ran my fingers over my thigh and looked at them, red with blood. I looked up at him in alarm.

"It's okay, that's normal," he said.

As I stood I looked down on the sheets, a small circle of red and my face flushed the same colour with embarrassment. Laughing he took my hand and led me to the bathroom. I desperately need to pee and crossed my legs. He turned on the faucet, letting the room fill with steam from the water filling the bath. I jigged about.

"I need to pee," I said.

"So, pee," he replied, as he poured some bubble bath under the running water.

I stood unsure of what to do.

"Evelyn, I've just had my tongue in you, you came in my mouth. It's a bit late to be embarrassed to pee in front of me," he said.

I covered my face with my hands while he laughed, holding back a giggle myself. Lifting the toilet seat, I sat and peed. When the bath was full, he held out his hand and helped me into the water. He climbed in behind me, wrapping his arms around my chest, his legs either side of mine as we squeezed into his narrow tub. The hot water stung and I winced as I settled down and relaxed back against him.

"I'm sorry, I didn't do, you know, anything to you," I cringed as I spoke.

"You did the ultimate, Evelyn, you gave your virginity to me," he replied, silencing me.

One hand slid down my stomach, the other caressed a breast. Whether it was the heat of the water opening my pores or the skill of his touch but my body responded immediately to it. His fingers slid through my soft hair just either side of my clitoris, already swollen and still tender. He gently squeezed causing a shot of electricity to fire through me. I let my head fall back on his chest as his fingers worked their magic. My hands gripped his thighs as the most delicious feelings flooded through me. I moaned with desire and felt his smile in my neck.

"You are so responsive," he said.

Not entirely understanding what he meant I relaxed and just enjoyed it. I had never been able to produce anywhere near these feelings myself, but I wanted to feel what he was doing. I moved my hand to cover his, to feel what his fingers were doing to me. He removed his and placed it over mine.

"You do it," he whispered.

I was too far gone to feel any shame, too far down the line to stop and with his fingers guiding mine, I brought myself to my second ever orgasm. Trying to calm my breathing after, I started to laugh, it wasn't long before he joined in. It was a wonderful sound, his laughter, a sound I would treasure and remember for many years to come. With the water cooling we climbed out of the bath, he wrapped a rather scratchy towel around me before placing one around his waist and we made our way back to the bedroom and dressed. My stomach rumbled reminding me it was long past lunchtime and that I hadn't eaten. Rocco took my hand, led me downstairs and to the kitchen. He had a small courtyard out back and a table with chairs. Opening the back door he ushered me out and told me to sit, he was going to prepare a late lunch for us. I rested my head back, closed my eyes and let my face soak up the last of the sun's rays before it moved behind the building beyond.

A short while later he returned with plates of olives, bread, oil, cheese and meats. He placed a carafe of red wine and two glasses on the table and we sat, drank, ate and chatted. He told me about his village, his family and their farm. He didn't talk about his father or his brother, just gave me general information. He also never mentioned the trouble that had brought his sister to America. I heard the ringing of a telephone and while he left to answer it, I cleared the dishes. I heard him speaking from the hallway.

"For fuck sake, Sammy, I'm busy. Can't you deal with it? You're a fucking liability. I'll be there in half an hour, try not to fuck up in that time."

I had never heard him curse that much before and the tone of his voice was so different to when he spoke to me. He was authoritative, angry at having been disturbed, I guessed. He strode back into the kitchen as I was drying the last of the plates. Placing his arms around my waist he pulled me into his chest.

"I have to go, business," he said.

I nodded, placed the dishcloth on the side and followed him to the front door. I collected my bag that had been left there and climbed in the car. He drove with one hand, the fingers of the other laced with mine. As we pulled up outside my house, I noticed the upstairs curtain twitch, Maria would have heard the car arrive. He placed his fingers under my chin and pulled my face towards him. He tasted of red wine but his kiss was all too brief.

"I'll see you tomorrow, what time do you finish work?" he asked.

"Five, normally."

"Okay, I'll see you at five then, I'll pick you up."

With that, I exited the car and watched him drive away. The reality of what had happened hit me then. A huge smile made my cheeks ache and I wrapped my arms around myself. The front door opened and Joey bounded down the steps. I picked him up with a squeal and swung him around. His little laugh was infectious and I laughed with him. Carrying him back inside I handed him over to Alana, the housekeeper. She was proving to be a godsend, staying overnight when papa was away and Joey was hugely attached to her. I followed her into the kitchen, she had prepared dinner, it was just a case of putting the lasagne in the oven a little later on. I enquired after Maria, other than for meals she hadn't left her room. I decided to pop in and see if she wanted to chat. I knocked on her door before gently opening it and popping my head through.

"Hi, do you fancy some company?" I asked.

She looked up from yet another book. There wasn't the sparkle in her eye I had seen the previous day, it was obviously a down time for her. She looked at me before gently shaking her head.

"It's okay, Maria, another time," I said before retreating.

I was going to have a serious chat with my father when he returned. Maria needed help for her mood swings, perhaps she was scared to leave the house, but whatever was wrong, it wasn't healthy. She was started to lose her natural olive skin tones, she looked so pale and although she seemed to sleep a lot, she was displaying dark circles under her eyes. She was only sixteen, soon to be seventeen, and she looked like an old woman.

****

The following day I headed for work. I felt different, I felt like a woman. I had studied myself in the mirror that morning, I didn't look different, except for that stupid grin I couldn't stop but there was a definite change in me. I wanted to share my news with someone and I missed Maria or having a close girlfriend, someone I could gossip and laugh with. I wanted to dance around and tell them, I had sex and it was wonderful. I spent the day as normal, answering the calls, tidying the office and trying to get the filing under control. It seemed Mr Philips hadn't a grasp on the alphabet yet. He was erratic, forgetful but fun to work for. I was starting to learn a little about the import business and it wasn't long before I noticed my father's name on bits of paper. I gathered that my father seemed to be 'investing' in Richmond Inc., he was certainly putting money in on a regular basis. I watched the clock tick so slowly from four until five and just before, I headed off to the restroom to refresh my makeup and tidy my hair.

Exactly at five Rocco walked into the reception. It was a sight that brought a smile to my face, he was dressed in a black T-shirt that moulded around every muscle and jeans. He gave me a wink. Mr Philips had rushed from his office and screeched to a halt just before colliding with him.

"Rocco, I wasn't expecting you," he said.

"I'm not here for you," Rocco replied.

I looked between them, the tension in the room tangible. I noticed the nervousness of Mr Philips. I coughed, clearing my throat and both looked at me. Rocco's face softened and I gathered my bag before rounding the desk. I bade a goodnight to Mr Philips as we left the office.

"What was that all about?" I asked.

"Nothing, business," Rocco replied.

I left it at that. My father always used that answer when he didn't want to discuss anymore and I was reminded of exactly who Rocco was. He took my hand as he led me to the car. We drove a little way out of the city and arrived at the driveway of a rather large and imposing house. Pulling up at the front, he turned in his seat.

"I have to collect my sister, she needs to return to Italy tomorrow. I thought she could come to dinner with us, you can get to know each other," he said.

As he finished his sentence she came out of the house. I watched as Rocco left the car and spoke to her, her head darting to look in as he had obviously told her I was in the car. She climbed into the back.

"Evelyn, I'm Adriana, it's good to meet you," she said in broken English.

"It's good to meet you too," I replied.

As Rocco got in the car she started to speak to him, in her dialect. I couldn't follow.

"English, or Italian, Adriana," he said.

"I'm sorry, Evelyn, sometimes I forget. Rocco, mamma has been on the phone, she wants you to call."

"I will, later," he replied, agitated.

We arrived at a pizzeria with a lovely courtyard out the back where we sat in the sun and ate. I watched Rocco and his sister chat back and forth. They included me in their conversation but I was also content to let them have this time. If I had known Adriana was to return to Italy the following day I would have told Rocco to spend the time alone with her. They looked remarkably similar and had I not known she was younger, they could have passed for twins. Both had those hazel eyes, lighter than mine. She had long, straight hair that shone as she moved and it caught the sun's rays. Every now and then she would revert to her dialect and Rocco would scold her. Every region in Italy had its own dialect and that's what Adriana was fluent in. Even though I could speak Italian, there would be phrases and words that would differ and sometimes I struggled to understand. The more remote the village the less likely they would speak English. I would smile at Adriana and she would roll her eyes every time her brother told her off. At one point, he left us to visit the restroom.

"I'm glad you're dating my brother, Evelyn. He must have been so lonely here. I know your family took him in but it's lovely to see him with a girlfriend," she said.

Had he told her I was his girlfriend? I assumed I was and if Adriana thought it too, hopefully that was the case. We hadn't mentioned the time I had seen her cry and I didn't bring up the conversation I'd had with Rocco about his family and their troubles. We chatted about DC, she had been able to do a couple of tourist trips, one to the White House and Capitol Hill and she gushed about it. The thing she loved the most was the abundance of clothes stores. I made a promise that I would send a couple of things out to her, there wasn't the amount of choice back home, she had told me. I really liked her, she talked about me visiting and how her mother would love to meet me. Rocco returned before she could make plans.

"You must bring Evelyn home, Rocco, meet mamma," she said, draining the last of her wine.

He stared at her without answering.

"Come on, it's time to go," he said.

It was clear that he was agitated as he strode to the car, leaving us trailing in his wake. I wasn't sure exactly what had upset him but decided not to ask, not while Adriana was still with us. She seemed oblivious to it, chatting all the way back to the cousin's house. He pulled on the front drive and without getting out, turned in his seat.

"I'll collect you later, drive you to the airport," he said.

She reached forward to kiss his cheek and mine before climbing out, waving and heading for the front door. He slumped slightly, sighing before he started the car and pulled away. I rested my hand on his thigh and we drove back in silence. The evening was still young and I hoped he wasn't planning on taking me straight home. I was thankful when he took the turn towards his house. He was still brooding when we arrived and he turned off the engine. We sat in silence for a minute or two before he took a deep breath and turned towards me.

"Sorry, I don't like that she's going home. I wanted her, and my mother, to come here, to leave the farm but they won't."

"Will your uncle look after them?" I asked.

"Yes, but I know they would be safer here. Come on, I don't want to talk about them anymore, it will spoil the evening."

We made our way to the house and once inside he pulled me into his arms.

"What do you want to do?" he asked.

I smiled up at him, raised my eyebrows and thankfully, his mood lifted and he laughed. Taking my hand, he led me to his bedroom. The bed was made this time, the room tidy and as he kicked off his shoes, I bunched his T-shirt in my hands and raised it over his head. I kissed him as he undid the buttons of my blouse, pushing it from my shoulders. We were desperate to rid each other of our clothes. He unclipped my bra and cupped a breast, his head bending to take the nipple in his mouth. As he did I popped the button on my trousers, letting them fall and stepped out of them. I clasped his head pulling his mouth to mine. This time I walked him backwards to the bed, I pushed at his chest until he fell, laughing. While he lay I slowly pulled down my panties, standing naked before him. He reached forward, grabbed my hand and pulled me down to lie on top of him. I loved the feel of his skin on mine, I loved the feel of his erection pushing through his jeans into my stomach and I ground myself against him. His moan caused a tightening in my stomach, just the notion that I was affecting him this much caused my heart to flutter, my breath to catch. I undid his jeans pulling them over his hips. His erection strained against his tight black shorts and I hooked my fingers either side, sliding them down to free him. I leant down and kissed his navel, I let my tongue travel down in that wonderful trail of hair until I found what I wanted. I wasn't sure how well I was going to do this but I wanted to try, I wanted him in my mouth, to taste him. My tongue played over the tip of his cock, tasting a small bead of fluid that had escaped. It wasn't unpleasant and I took him in my mouth. I heard him wince, then laugh.

"Gently," he said.

I used my tongue as a barrier against my teeth and sucked him, like I would a popsicle. Judging by the fisting of his hands in my hair, by the way he raised his hips each time I took him further in my mouth and the moans, I must have been doing something right. However, it wasn't long before my jaw ached. I replaced my mouth with my hand gently squeezing.

"Show me how you like this," I whispered.

His hand covered mine and he guided me. I watched his face the whole time, his eyes were closed and his lips parted. Soon enough I got an idea of what he wanted. I pulled his hand away and continued on my own, watching with fascination the changes to his face, the tightening in his stomach muscles. I upped the pace and used my other hand to cup his balls, rolling them around, using my nails to gently scratch that smooth skin just behind. I watched as his hands gripped the bedding and I felt his cock twitching in mine. A hot, milky fluid erupted from him, coating my hand, his stomach, at the same time as he called out my name. I smiled, pleased with myself, I was obviously a quick learner.

He opened his eyes and smiled at me, except I wasn't quite sure what to do now. He reached across to his nightstand and plucked some tissues from a box, handing them to me with a laugh, I guess he had seen the look of confusion on my face.

"Your turn," he said as he pulled me towards him.

I lay on my back as he propped himself on his elbow at my side. His hand trailed down my stomach and I parted my legs, ready for him. His fingers brushed against my clitoris, sending those wonderful shock waves through my stomach before pushing one then two inside me. I was still a little sore, there was a little burn but the feeling of his fingers inside me, stroking, was indescribable. My legs quivered, my heart rate increased and warmth spread over me. And then he did something, he pushed against a certain spot inside me and it was as if my body exploded around him. I cried out, I arched my back and I fell apart.

Before I had gathered my wits, processed what had happened, Rocco moved on top of me, he placed a condom on himself and pushed into me. I wrapped my legs around his waist, my arms around his neck, raising my hips with every thrust. He growled into my neck, the sound reverberating through my body and he fucked me hard.

****

I didn't see Rocco the following day, he had already told me that he had business to take care of and we were expecting my father back. I sat in the garden room after work, listening to Joey playing outside and thought about the last couple of days. Whenever I thought of Rocco, that quivering in my stomach returned. I wanted to spend every moment in bed with him and I missed his touch. We also needed to have that conversation. Were we a couple? Would we tell my father? In the back of my mind though, I knew I was holding back on that as much as he was.

I heard the front door open, the sound of voices and knew my father had returned. His laughter brought a smile to my lips and I rose to greet him. I was pushed to one side as Joey ran through the room and into his father's arms, squealing as he was lifted and swung around. With Joey on his hip, my father pulled me into an embrace.

"Look at my beautiful children," he said to the men surrounding him.

I rolled my eyes, this was always his response when he hadn't seen us for a couple of days. The men surrounding him had known me most of my life, but they laughed and played along. The last person to enter the house was Rocco, I smiled as I saw him and then frowned, he completely ignored me. He didn't even look my way choosing instead to ruffle Joey's hair as he made his way into my father's home office. That hurt. Taking Joey from my father I headed back to the kitchen; papa would want coffee. Piling cups and a coffee jug on a tray I made to enter the office, the door was slightly ajar. I was pulled up short at the words I heard.

"So, Rocco, I hear you have a girlfriend," I heard my father say.

"No, just having a bit of fun, Joe, no one important," came the reply.

An involuntary gasp left my lips and I saw Rocco look towards the door. I pushed it open with my hip and stumbled in. Placing the tray on the desk I kept my head bowed, my face blistering as coffee spilt and burnt my hand.

"Always so clumsy," my father said, tutting.

I rushed to the kitchen, running the cold water over my hand and trying desperately to not let tears falls. So I was just a 'bit of fun', was I? His words stung. I could hear him laugh at whatever was being said and all I wanted to do was to get out, to not hear him. I crept past the door, taking my jacket from the hook and left the house.

I walked with no destination in mind but somehow found myself looking up at the large oak doors of the church. Making my way around the side, I headed for my mother's grave. I missed her, all the time, but right now I wanted nothing more than to feel her arms around me, to comfort me and to whisper soothing words in my ear. I wanted to talk to her about what was going on in my body and in my mind. I sat on the grass, the dampness soaking into my jeans and let it all pour out. I don't know for how long I sat, but the sun had set and the street lamps cast an eerie orange glow over the cemetery. I rose, brushed the grass from my backside and pulled my jacket around me, the temperature had started to drop as the night drew in.

I knew my father would be anxious. Me being out, alone, at night was not something he liked. Although I knew I would be safe, people knew who I was, no one would harm me for fear of my family's retaliation. I walked as quickly as I could back towards the house. The lights were blazing, the front door open and as I made my way along the path I heard someone call out.

"She's here."

My father rushed to the front door, he pulled me by arms and into his chest.

"Where have you been? You know you don't go out alone, at night," he said.

"Sorry papa, I just wanted a bit of fresh air. I'm fine, nothing to worry about."

"Nothing to worry about! One minute you're here, the next gone," he waved his arms dramatically in the air and I sighed.

He turned to Jonathan, "Go find Rocco, tell him she's back."

So Rocco had been sent or had he chosen to go find me? I wouldn't ask but now felt bad for worrying my father. I placed my hand on his cheek and smiled at him.

"Papa, I'm nineteen in a week, a big girl now," I said.

"You will always be my baby, *bella*, don't forget that," he replied.

"I'm tired, papa, I think I'll head off to bed."

I wanted to be alone and in my room before Rocco returned, I wasn't ready to see him yet, his words still swimming through my mind.

Chapter Three

My father seemed to be busier than usual, I saw him briefly in the evenings when I returned from work. I hadn't seen or heard from Rocco in three days. I missed him, terribly. I missed listening to his voice, the softness when he whispered to me. I missed his scent, the mix of cigarette and aftershave and I missed his body, the feel of him under my hands. As the days had moved on, I began to understand why he had said what he had. I knew he wouldn't have told my father about us but he didn't need to refer to us in that way. But I didn't have the confidence to make the first approach. I could have visited my father at his office, Rocco would have been there but to have him ignore me again would have been torture.

I hung on every word my father said, listening of any mention of him. I tried many times to drop his name into the conversation. A couple of times my father looked at me, his eyebrows furrowed together in question and I worried that I may have alerted him to my feelings. And on the fourth day, he came to me.

It was a hot night, I had thrown the sheets from the bed and slept in a thin T-shirt, my body covered with a light film of sweat. I was woken, with a start, by a hand being placed over my mouth.

"Shush, it's just me," Rocco said.

As my eyes adjusted to the low light I saw him, kneeling at the side of the bed. He looked dishevelled and I could smell liquor on his breath. I nodded, letting him know I wasn't about to scream.

"What are you doing here?" I whispered.

"I couldn't stay away, I tried, but I can't," he replied.

He sat on the edge of the bed and ran his hand through his hair. I reached to turn on the bedside lamp. His eyes were bloodshed, his hair ruffled.

"You're drunk," I said.

"No, I was but not now. I needed to see you."

"You've ignored me all week, why now? It's the middle of the night," I said.

"I'm sorry, Evelyn. We need to talk but I think your father knows, he has kept me away from the house. I've tried to find a reason to come here and he seems to be blocking it."

I sat up, as I did the T-shirt rose, exposing my panties. He rested his hand on my thigh, his thumb just brushing the edge of the plain white cotton and I closed my eyes, briefly.

"No, if you want to talk, that's what we'll do," I said, pushing his hand a little way down.

"Not here, Ev, if he catches me in your bedroom, that will be it for us."

I nodded.

"Tomorrow then, find an excuse to pick me up from work. I'll tell papa that I'm going straight out, I won't be home for dinner."

His hand rested on the side of my face and he leant forwards, his lips just brushing mine.

"Tomorrow," he whispered.

He stood and left as silently as he had arrived. I lay for hours afterwards unable to get back to sleep and watched the sun rise, already counting down the hours until I would see him again.

****

The day dragged unbelievably slowly, I watched the clock yet the hands didn't seem to have moved from the last time I studied it. I was testy, lack of sleep didn't agree with me and I snapped a couple of times at Mr Philips when he lost yet another round of papers I had given him to sign. He had asked me if I was okay, I apologised but as much as I needed someone to confide in, it wouldn't be him. I had told my father that I was meeting with an old school friend after work, we would grab a pizza and they would drop me home, no need for a car. He seemed pleased that I was socialising and I felt just terrible lying to him.

When five o'clock finally arrived I thought it best to wait outside. I didn't want Mr Philips to innocently mention that Rocco had visited the office to my father, should he see him. I spotted his car and made my way over. When I settled into the passenger seat, Rocco started the car and drove off, no kiss hello, no touching. We drove for a few miles in silence before I watched him start to relax. As we hit the freeway, heading towards Great Falls, he took my hand in his. He gave me a smile and I too relaxed. The car windows were open, the breeze ruffled my hair and as the surrounding areas became more green, more rural, I took some deep calming breaths.

"Where are we going?" I asked.

"Somewhere hopefully no one knows us," he said with a chuckle.

He pulled alongside a small restaurant, the darkened windows not giving away what was inside, and I climbed out of the car. The restaurant was like stepping back in time. A cool interior, for which I was thankful, housed small wooden tables with chequered cloths. All the tables were set for two and along one side, larger booths. Rocco took my hand and led me to the furthest one from the door. At this early hour, the restaurant was empty save for one other couple sitting in the window. They didn't acknowledge us and we settled down, sitting side by side.

A waiter appeared with menus and once he left, Rocco turned to face me.

"I can't be sure but I think your father knows something. He has had me running all over the place this week. Whenever I've needed to speak to him, he arranges to be at the office, never at home."

"Do you think he would really be upset about us?" I asked.

He shrugged his shoulders. "I honestly don't know, Evelyn. I do know that he often talks about you meeting a lawyer or a doctor. I doubt he would think I was good enough for you."

"That's just stupid. It's my choice who I see, and come on, can you imagine if I brought a *lawyer* home, a man of the law." I laughed at the irony of that.

"What do you know, Ev? About what your father does?" he asked.

"Not everything, of course. I know what he does isn't legal though. I've seen the bundles of money, I've seen the guns, Rocco. And my mother confirmed it when she said that, although she loved papa, this wasn't a life she wanted for me."

When I said those words I knew I had said the wrong thing. Pain flashed through his eyes and I reached out to hold his hand.

"I can't help who I fall in love with," I whispered.

He didn't speak, he didn't tell me he loved me back but he didn't let go of my hand either. He squeezed, running his thumb over my knuckles. He went to say something but I placed my fingers over his lips and just shook my head. If he didn't love me, I didn't want to hear the words at that moment. I wanted just to have my fantasy for a little while longer. We scanned the menu, decided what we wanted and placed our order. Taking a sip of my wine I watched him. He was deep in thought, his jaw working from side to side, grinding.

"You'll have no teeth left if you keep doing that," I said.

He laughed and the tension seemed to lift. We chatted, me about my day at work and he told me about Jonathan's new love. Patricia had come to meet Jonathan from work, surprising everyone there. Father didn't encourage people to come unannounced, so I laughed when Rocco told me there was a thirty-second scramble to clear papers and *things* she shouldn't be seeing. I didn't ask what *things* he was talking about. I had learnt a long time ago it was best not to know what when on in that office. But I liked Jonathan, he had worked for my father ever since I could remember and I was pleased he had a girlfriend.

The longer we sat, the more relaxed he became and the more affectionate he was. He stroked my thigh causing my stomach to tighten. I had no doubt he knew the effect he was having on me, he would glance sideways, giving me a smile or a wink of his eye. I pushed all thoughts of my father and the past few days to the back of mind, I was determined I was going to make this relationship, or whatever it was, work. I wanted it and I believed I could talk my father round.

With the meal over he held out his hand and we left the restaurant. Instead of heading to the car, we took a walk through the neighbouring parkland. He held my hand until we came to a grassy hill where we sat and he placed his arm around my shoulders, pulling me close.

"I don't know what the future is, Ev, I want to be honest with you," he said.

"Please, don't say..." He cut me off.

"Hear me out. I don't even have a visa to be here, did you know that? Your father's influence means I haven't already been picked up and sent packing. And that's what bothers me. If I don't have his support, I'm gone. Do you understand what I'm saying?"

"If you want him to know, Rocco, I'll talk to him. He's never refused me."

"And if you're wrong? I can't let myself fall in love, Evelyn, because I'm too scared that it will be taken away. But I can't let you go either," he said, softly.

We sat in silence for a while. Maybe I was desperate but I wanted whatever he would give me, for now. He had said he couldn't let me go, that meant he felt something, didn't it? He might not want to love me but I believed he did.

"Take me home, Rocco, to your house," I said.

Holding hands, we made our way back to the car, the tension mounting the closer we got to his house. I squirmed in my seat, already aroused and trying to find some release. His hand would rub up and down my thigh and I sunk a little in my seat forcing it higher. I could feel the dampness soaking through my panties, my nipples erect and chafing against the material of my bra. And I could see his erection, straining against the front of his jeans. I reached over, rubbing my hand over the bulge. He sucked in a breath and his foot pressed down harder on the gas pedal.

He parked the car, haphazardly, grabbed my hand and dragged me to the front door. Opening it, his mouth found mine and we stumbled through, he kicked it shut behind him. It took less than a minute to discard our clothes, leaving a trail up the stairs. It took a few seconds for him to rip open that foil packet and place a condom on himself and just a few seconds more before he was where I needed him to be, inside me. My hands raked down his hard back, my moans grew louder with every thrust. I couldn't get him deep enough, I wanted more of him.

"Harder, deeper," I panted.

He pulled out of me, taking me by surprise and my eyes sprang open.

"Get on your knees," he said, his voice husky and commanding.

Before I knew what was happening, he was kneeling behind me and slammed into me so fast it took my breath away. I gripped the bedding to hold myself upright but as he started to move, the sensation was far greater than ever before. I pushed myself back against him, wanting him deeper still. He gripped my hips digging his fingers in as he thrust faster. I screamed out as the most intense orgasm ripped through me. My arms shook and I fell to my elbows, my legs quivered. I felt him shudder, his grip tighten as he cried out himself.

My legs gave way and I fell, face down on the bed. I struggled to get my breath and licked the beads of sweat that had formed on my upper lip. I could hear Rocco's fast breathing, I could feel his hot breath as he lay on top of me, his chest to my back, his face buried in the side of my neck. I could feel his heart pounding in perfect time with mine.

Then I giggled, the giggle turned into a laugh. I was trying to bury my face in the sheets to quieten the sound although I knew there was no one to hear us. Hysteria took over me. The laughter became sobs, big, stomach aching sobs. The past week, the hopelessness of our situation, our relationship, hit me all at once. Rocco rolled to one side, he pulled me into an embrace and whispered soothing words in my ear. He held me tight to his chest until my sobs died down to a whimper. My eyes had started to close, the exhaustion of my outburst catching me unaware. The last thing I felt was him stroking the hair from my sodden cheeks.

I woke with a start, the room was dark and I fumbled in the dim moonlight to see the time on my watch.

"Shit, Rocco, wake up, it's gone midnight," I said, shaking his arm.

Although I didn't have a curfew, my father would still be waiting up for me. He would not retire until he knew I was safely home and getting home was going to be difficult. Rocco could hardly drive me to the front door and the enquiry I would get if I walked would be unbearable. We scrabbled around the room, the hallway, the stairs to find our clothes, doing the last of my buttons up as I climbed into his car. I used the vanity mirror to check my hair, to wipe the smudge of mascara from my cheek and the journey home took half the time. Rocco stopped the car a couple of doors down from my house.

"I'll walk you," he said.

"No, papa might see you. I'll be fine from here."

As I reached to open the door, he wrapped his hand around my neck, pulling me to him for a deep, last kiss. The uncertainty of my reception made me shiver and I wrapped my jacket tight around me as I walked just the short distance to the house. I turned and gave what I thought was a discrete wave just as I headed up the path. The sound of someone clearing their throat caused me to grip my hand to my chest. When I peered into the shadows beside the front door, the lit end of a cigar glowed, illuminating Jonathan.

"Jesus, you scared me," I said, walking forwards.

"Well actually, it's Jonathan. Jesus left a few minutes ago," he said.

I tutted and shook my head, my heart beat finally returning to normal.

"Was that Rocco, Evelyn?" he asked.

"He just gave me a lift, he was in town and my friend wanted to get a cab to a bar," I said, stuttering a little.

Lying did not come easily to me, my heart thudded in my chest.

"Then why not walk you to the door?" he replied.

I had no answer for that and we just stared at each other.

"Please, Jonathan, don't say anything, not yet. I will tell papa but not just yet."

"Evelyn, I don't think I have to tell you how your father would react, do I?"

"Why? What's so wrong with Rocco?"

"It's not what's wrong with him, it's more about what your father wants for you."

"Jonathan, I'm nineteen, I don't exactly have men knocking down my front door to date me. They're too scared of my father. My father, you guys, this *business* you're in means I am unlikely to meet the doctor, the lawyer, the Mr Respectable, don't you think?" I replied, angrily.

I slumped down on the step. Throwing the end of his cigar in the bushes, he came and sat beside me.

"He just wants the best for you," he said, gently.

"And what about what I want? I would have loved to have had a normal life, to have friends, but I don't. This is it, Jonathan. You go home at the end of the day to your normal girlfriend, I live this life twenty-four hours, seven days a week. If I have to wait for the best, for the one papa will approve of, I'll grow old, lonely."

We fell silent for a moment.

"I love him," I said, quietly.

"Does he love you?"

"I don't know. He's scared of what father will do, he's scared of loving me."

Jonathan sighed. "Just be careful, okay."

I smiled my thanks and headed inside, Jonathan following and closing the front door behind him. I called out to my father that I was back and found him in the kitchen, tasting something from a wooden spoon.

"Papa, what are you doing?" I asked.

"Driving the car, Evelyn, what does it look like? I'm hungry. Jonathan hand me those plates."

My father was stirring a tomato sauce and on the side were two plates of pasta, he spooned the sauce over and asked me if I wanted any. I was starving, despite having eaten earlier and dished some for myself. We sat and I listened to my father probe Jonathan about his new girlfriend, thankful I wasn't in that seat.

Chapter Four

Each day that I spent with Rocco became increasingly difficult. It hurt so much inside that I was lying to my father, concocting stories about imaginary friends that I would dine out with, that I would go to the movie theatre with. But the time I spent with him was wonderful, was worth the deceit and I loved him more and more each day. There was one thing I wanted though, more than anything. I wanted to wake up next to him in the morning, to sleep the night in his arms having made love. I had never stayed out a whole night before. It was getting later that I returned but still, my father would be up, waiting for me to safely get home.

"Papa, a friend has asked me to stay over, we're going out to dinner then a late movie," I said over breakfast.

"Stay overnight? Which friend is this, Evelyn?" he asked.

"Oh you know, Carmella, from school. We just became friends again."

"Carmella? No, I don't think I know that one."

"I'm sure you do, papa, anyway, I thought I would just let you know, so you didn't wait up."

I wasn't going to ask, to give him the opportunity to say no. I was too old to be told what to do but this was still his house, I lived under his roof and his rules. I glanced

59

quickly at him. His eyes bored straight at me and I knew he didn't believe me. I tried my hardest to just smile and made to clear the table.

"Evelyn, is there anything you want to tell me?" he asked.

"Like what, papa?" I said, feigning innocence.

"Is it a boy?"

"Be a funny name for a boy," I replied with a laugh.

"If it's a boy, Evelyn, I would rather you told me the truth."

"When I date someone, I hope he'll be a man, but I'll let you know."

"Mmmm, if you're mother was here...," he didn't finish the sentence.

"If my mother was here, she would be excited that I was going out, boy or girl. Be happy for me, papa, please."

I rose and cleared the table, my cheeks burning at bringing my mother into my web of lies, perhaps it was time for confession. Since getting my job I had only been able to help out at the church one evening a week, and I felt guilty that all the time I was there I was wishing I was somewhere else. I didn't see Rocco every night of the week but at least three or four times, sometimes just for an hour or so. When he came to the house, he was polite but distant and I would often catch Jonathan looking at us, seeing if we gave anything away.

Jonathan became a close ally, not that he openly encouraged us but if Rocco had to drop me home and Jonathan was visiting, he would distract my father long enough for us to say our goodnight. Whether he ever spoke to Rocco about us, I didn't know. He proved his support for me one day, getting me out of a very sticky moment. I was washing the dishes after lunch, my father sitting at the table with Jonathan, discussing a building project he was about to embark on.

"Whose jewellery is this?" he asked. I had left it on the side while I had my hands in the sink.

"Mine, papa," I replied.

I wore my mother's engagement ring but I had a new item. A simple gold chain bracelet that Rocco had presented to me a couple of nights previous.

"The ring was your mothers, but the bracelet? I don't remember her ever wearing something like that."

I stilled, not sure what to say. I doubted my father would believe me if I told him I had bought it. I would buy my own clothes and shoes, but never a bracelet.

"I don't know, Joe. Didn't we get this in payment for a debt?" Jonathan said.

"What this cheap thing? Whoever it was couldn't have owed much," my father said, laughing.

I turned from the sink, drying my hands on the dishcloth. I wanted to snatch the bracelet from him. Maybe it was cheap, I didn't know but I believed it was a way of Rocco telling me he loved me. You don't buy jewellery for your girlfriend if you didn't love them. However, I sat, held out my hand to receive the bracelet and put it back on. Jonathan gave me a quick smile.

I kissed my father on the top of his head as I passed by, reminding him that I was staying out that night and headed to the front door. I had arranged to meet Rocco that afternoon at the church and with a small overnight bag I left the house. I hadn't told Rocco that I intended to stay the night, I wanted it to be a surprise. As I rounded the corner and the church came into view, I saw his car. He was standing outside, leaning against the door, smoking a cigarette and when he saw me, he threw it to the ground and started to walk towards me.

"What's this?" he asked, taking my bag from me.

"I'm staying the night, with you."

Tracie Podger

"Okay, how did you manage that?"

"Papa thinks I'm with Carmella, someone I knew from school."

We walked to the car and he opened the door, placing the bag on the back seat before helping me in. We drove the short distance to his house. For the first time I felt like we were a real couple, doing grown up things as we stood side by side in the kitchen making coffee, as we snuggled on the sofa to watch a movie. A small pang of sadness hit me that this all had to be done in secret. What I wouldn't give to be able to walk in public holding his hand, to be able to snuggle with him at my own house, to sit and chat with my family about him. Every time the phone rang or we heard a noise outside the house, we were jumping from our seats, waiting with bated breath for a knock on the door. It was quite normal for one of the guys working for my father to call on Rocco if they needed him and I would be rushed to the bedroom, to hide. Sometimes we would laugh, sometimes I would sigh, wishing it was different.

"I need to take a shower," I said, after the movie had finished.

I headed upstairs, collecting my overnight bag on the way. Although I hadn't told Rocco, I had visited the doctors the previous month, started to take the contraceptive pill and I was fanatical about taking it at the same time each day. Popping a little pill in my mouth, dry swallowing, I started to undress. I shivered as I stepped under the jets, not quite warm enough and let the cool water run over my body. As I lathered body wash in my hands I heard the bathroom door open, I watched the silhouette strip of any clothing before the glass door was opened. Already aroused, Rocco pulled me to his chest, the water dripping down our faces and catching on our lips, our tongues, as he kissed me.

I ran my soapy hands over his chest, down his stomach and clasped his hard cock, gently massaging before lowering myself to my knees. Letting the water rinse the soap suds first, I took him in my mouth, all the way to the back of my throat. His hands tangled in my wet hair as his hips thrust forwards in time with me. My hands reached behind and grabbed his ass, squeezing and kneading. His moans dictated the pace. I loved the taste of him, the silkiness of his skin on my lips as I pulled back, all the way to the tip and then down, as far as I could, each time testing my limits.

"Ev, I'm gonna come," he said as he tried to pull my head away.

I sucked harder, milking him, letting his salty fluid pulse to the back of my throat as he cried out loud. As his body shuddered I slowly released him, my tongue licking away the last of his come. It wasn't the taste that I liked, it was when I looked up at him, through my wet eyelashes and saw his face, the pure ecstasy that I had created. He pulled me, roughly, to my feet, his mouth crashing down on mine as his tongue forced my teeth apart. One hand gripped my thigh, raising my leg to his waist while the other held my throat, tilting my head up to his. His body pinned me to the wall and his cock hardened against my stomach.

"Fuck me, now," I whispered.

"I need a..."

"No, you don't," I cut him off. "I went on the pill."

He picked me up, my legs wrapped around his waist and with one hand he slid open the shower door. Resting my ass against the sink, he pushed into me. Goose bumps covered my skin, not just from the cooling water but from the sensation of having him inside me, of having his wet chest slide against mine, of having his lips on my neck, my face and of having his hands grip my hips so hard I knew I would bruise.

My orgasm came quick, hard, and I threw my head back and screamed out his name. His fingers teased my clitoris as his cock pounded leaving me with a delicious ache in my stomach. But he wasn't done yet. Pulling out, he turned and bent me forwards, I held onto the sink as he entered me from behind. One of his hands wrapped around my hair, forcing my head up and when I did, I looked at his reflection in the mirror. His eyes were closed, his teeth biting his lower lip, his brow furrowed in concentration. I watched him come. I saw the shuddering to his stomach, how tightly he screwed his eyes shut, how he parted his lips to draw in a gasp of air. Then, when he was done, how he opened his eyes and looked straight back at me, a wicked smile on his lips.

I rested my head down on the cool basin, getting my breathing under control as Rocco lent forwards and placed a gentle kiss on my back.

"Wow," he said.

I giggled, wow indeed. I could feel a wetness on my thighs and looking, I saw his come gently make its escape. This was something new. I reached for some tissues to clean myself, mildly embarrassed before heading back into the now cold jets of the shower. A quick scrub later I was wrapped in a soft towel and sitting on his bed.

Rocco was leaning against his open window, in just a pair of jeans, smoking his cigarette. He looked pensive and I wondered what was going through his mind. He was often quiet, contemplating, after sex and I let him be. My tummy grumbled reminding me it was dinner time. Pulling on a T-shirt and a pair of his shorts, I made my way downstairs, I wanted to cook him dinner.

I was busy in the kitchen, laying out bowls of pasta when he came in. Moving around me, he collected glasses, wine and plates. It felt so comfortable, so normal to be in his kitchen, I imagined this would be our life if we lived together. If we could summon up the courage to tell my father, perhaps we could. He was still topless, just in his jeans and as we sat, my eyes wandered over his tattoos.

"What do they all mean?" I asked.

"What?"

"Your tattoos, do they have meanings?"

"Some, others are just designs I liked or drew myself. This one here," he said pointing to a dragon that snaked up his arm. "This means strength and courage, something I needed a long time ago."

"Will you tell me about it?" I asked.

He set his fork down and rested back in his chair.

"It was a month or so before I came here, to America, I think, when I was sat with my sister in the square, in my village. We were just watching the world go by when I saw him, one of the men that had taken my father and brother. I watched him sit with his friends, drinking coffee, laughing and grabbing for the waitress when she passed. I don't think I have ever felt such hatred, it was eating me inside. His face was all I had seen every time I closed my eyes. I knew it was him. He caught me staring and I knew he thought there was something familiar about me, but he couldn't place me, you know, when someone frowns at you?"

He paused to take a sip of his wine. I watched a pulse beat frantically in his neck and I placed my hand on his arm.

"You don't have to tell me anymore, Rocco, it's fine," I said. My words were ignored.

"I waited until he left then I followed him. I watched him walk into a house and I crept to the window to see. There was a young woman with him, he was shouting at her and she was crying. He slapped her face and she fell. I must have stepped on something, I don't know, but he looked towards the window. I ducked but he must have seen me.

It was all quiet for a little while and I started to move to the back of the house. I don't think I really knew what I was going to do but as I rounded the corner, I came face to face with him.

He went to grab me and we fought, I could hear the girl crying and saw her trying to pull him from me. She might have been his daughter, she looked too young to be his wife but he pushed her to the ground, again. She ran to the kitchen and came back with a knife, a fucking big knife. Maybe she had lost it, I don't know, but she was never going to get close enough to him to do anything with it. We all just stood, watching each other and somehow she managed to be standing next to me. He was laughing at her, goading her, "Fucking do it," he was shouting. I took the knife from her hands and did it myself."

He turned to look at me. "I stuck him right through his ribs, as far as I could and I watched him die."

"Oh, God," I said as I covered my mouth. I felt sick and rushed to the sink.

I heard the scrape of a chair as I retched, I felt him pull my hair to one side and rub my back. He reached for a glass, filled it with water and as I stood, the back of my hand wiping my mouth, he handed it to me.

"Sit, take a drink," he said, quietly.

"I'm sorry, it was just a shock, to hear you say that," I replied.

He shrugged his shoulders. "I haven't told anyone the full story. I ran, I left the girl there screaming and I ran home. My mother knew something was wrong, instantly. My hands were covered with his blood. She called my uncle, he called your father. I hid, in the grounds of the house for a few days. We had a small wooden building, for tools, I slept there every night. One evening though they came, I heard the shouting, calling my name but I stayed put, hiding out until they left. The next thing, I was on a plane."

"What would have happened, if you had stayed?" I asked.

"It was his friends that had come looking for me. You have to know, everyone knows everyone in the village, the girl must have described me, I don't know. Fucking amazing considering she was the one who went for him first. If they had caught me, I guess I wouldn't be sitting here now."

I couldn't put my finger on the description I wanted, to understand the expression on his face. It was a mixture of sadness, of remorse but more, resignation of what could have been, I guess.

"As much as I respected your mother, I knew she didn't want me at your house. But your father thought it was the safest place. No one would come for me at your home. I didn't like it though, I was putting you at risk."

He had turned to face me, my knees between his and his fingers tangled with my hair, smoothing a strand behind my ear.

"I saw how you looked at me, I knew," he whispered. "I needed to get out, to protect you."

"Those men wouldn't have dare come to my house," I said.

"Not from them, Evelyn, from me. I was in a bad place."

I raised my hands, placed them either side of his head and pulled him towards me. His kiss was tentative at first, loving even. He stood, held out his hand and walked me from the kitchen, up the stairs and to the bedroom. Silently he undressed me, lay me on the bed and then, well, then he made love to me.

He was gentle, he whispered words I didn't understand, he kissed the whole of my body. He held me in his arms as I came, giving in himself at the same time. I felt the wetness of his tears against my neck and I wrapped my arms around him as we both fell asleep, entwined, tangled, together.

Chapter Five.

I woke before the sun had risen. At some point during the night Rocco had untangled his legs from mine although his arm was still around my shoulders, my head resting on his chest as he lay on his back. I could hear his heartbeat, a steady rhythm that soothed me. The heat of his body was making me hot though. As gently as I could I slipped out of the bed, threw on the T-shirt I had found discarded on the floor and made my way downstairs. After making myself a coffee I sat and thought about the previous night. It shamed me to not have any particular feelings about what Rocco had done. I guessed, although on the fringes, I had grown up around this 'eye for an eye' code. Selfishly I was more excited about how he had treated me after. We hadn't fucked, we had made love, I had stayed the night. For me, this symbolised a *real* relationship. I had never mentioned how I felt after that first time and he had never responded. It was something left unsaid.

I felt two arms wrap around my waist as I stood at the sink, rinsing my coffee cup, it startled me and he laughed into my neck.

"I need to go out, will you stay here?" he whispered between kisses.

"Now? It's so early," I replied, then laughed. I sounded like his nagging wife.

"I won't be long, business," he said.

69

Turning in his arms I kissed him hard, giving him something he would want to return to. He left and I made my way back to the bedroom. I was wide awake there was no point in returning to bed. I showered and dressed, disappointed in one way to erase the smell of him from my body. I cleaned the bathroom, made the bed and tidied away his clothes. Looking in his closet, there was so little hanging there. It looked like it belonged to someone who wasn't planning on staying too long. Or, someone who hadn't the time to pack a suitcase before being bundled on a plane, I reminded myself. But that was a couple of years ago now. I pushed the thought down that had crept into my mind, perhaps he never intended on staying, my insecurities about us taking over.

I sat in his courtyard with another coffee and my book. The sun had risen and that little area was a trap for its rays. I watered his dying plants and generally busied myself playing house. It was a couple of hours later that he returned.

"Ciao," he said as he saw me sitting in the garden.

I rose to greet him, he smelled of cigarettes as he pulled me to him.

"Let me get you a coffee," I said.

As he sat, he said, "Mmmm, I could get used to this."

My heart skipped a beat, maybe, one day, I hoped.

I knew not to ask about his 'business', I had seen, far too many times, my father wave his hand, dismissing, should my mother had ever asked. In my world, ignorance was most definitely bliss. I watched through the window as he pulled his T-shirt over his head and stretched out his legs, resting back in this chair to catch the sun. Rummaging through my bag, I took my camera and snapped a shot of him through the glass. His eyes were shut, his face raised to the sky and a smile played on his lips. He had his hands behind his head and his biceps bulged, his stomach muscles were taught. It was a photo I would take to bed with me on lonely nights.

Taking pictures had become a new hobby, after receiving the camera for my nineteenth birthday a couple of months previously. My father had proudly presented it to me but I would have to be careful, he was as enthusiastic about seeing my pictures as I was. I would have to make sure when I had the film printed, I removed the one of Rocco.

Taking his coffee to him, I sat and picked up my book, letting him relax.

"What are you reading?" he asked.

I showed him the cover.

"Knights on white horses and all that shit, huh?"

"It's romance, Rocco, something us girls love."

He chuckled, "Well, come on over here, you can always ride me."

Giving me a cheeky grin, I couldn't help but laugh. I climbed on his lap, my knees either side of his legs and wrapped my arms around his neck. His hands ran up my thighs, pushing my shorts as far as they would go.

"You are so beautiful, Evelyn," he murmured as he nuzzled into my chest.

I kissed the top of his head and rested my cheek on his hair. He raised his head and kissed his way up my throat.

"It's been so good having you here, sleeping in my bed," he said.

"I know, I don't want to leave," I said with a sigh.

"Maybe it's time, Evelyn, we tell your father. You can move in with me."

"My father won't let me move in with you, even if he did approve of us."

"We'll see. There's something going on right now, though. I can't tell you, but in a few weeks, I will talk to him."

He saw my look of alarm.

"Your father is fine, it's just business that needs to be concluded, he will be in a happy place after, trust me."

I settled into his lap with a smile, the future was suddenly looking very rosy. He had to love me, he wouldn't want me to live with him otherwise, would he? It would be lovely to hear him say the words though. He hadn't mentioned marriage, just to live together. Perhaps I was jumping ahead of myself, living together would be wonderful, marriage could come after. I started to dream of my wedding day.

A banging on the front door startled us, Rocco leapt from the chair, holding me so I wouldn't fall to the ground. He placed his fingers to his lips, pointed to a corner in the yard. I nodded and backed into the shadows, out of view from the kitchen window. He pulled on his T-shirt and made his way to the front, closing the back door behind him. I could hear voices, laughing and saw Jonathan peep through the window. I shrunk back into the wall, as far as I could. The back door opened and Jonathan poked his head out.

"Want a glass of wine, Evelyn?" he asked.

I stepped forward. "You scared me, again," I said.

He laughed and made his way to the small table, followed by a stunning woman and Rocco.

"Evelyn, may I introduce Patricia?" he said, ever the gentleman.

"Hi, I'm really glad to meet you," she said, holding out her hand.

I took it, gave her a smile and returned the greeting. Rocco poured wine while we chatted. Patricia and Jonathan had been dating a few months and it seemed he was introducing her to his friends, our family. There was a wariness in everything that was said, she certainly asked some probing questions and whether she guessed we had dodged the answers or not, I wasn't sure.

"Joe doesn't know Evelyn is dating Rocco, so no mention of her being here, okay?" Jonathan said, gently, to her. "But, Ev, you might want to move your coat from the hallway."

Rocco didn't keep his distance, he sat beside me, his arm slung across the back of my seat, his fingers gently rubbing my back and I was pleased. Our first public display of being a couple. We chatted for an hour or so, the temperature dropped as the sun dipped down to the horizon.

"Ev, I think your father is expecting you back for dinner," Jonathan said.

I nodded, my perfect weekend coming to a close. I would have loved to have stayed longer but I could use Jonathan to give me a lift home, he lived not far from where I had told my father I was staying. I headed up to the bedroom to collect my things while Jonathan and Patricia headed for the car, to wait. Rocco followed me. Wrapping his arms around me, he hugged me.

"It's been a perfect weekend, Evelyn, thank you," he said.

His kiss was deep, wanting, his arms tightened around me as one hand snaked into my hair, holding my head to his. We were breathless as we parted.

"I'll see you in a couple of days?" I asked.

"Of course," he replied.

I didn't see him a couple of days later. In fact, I never saw him again.

Chapter Six

Two days had passed since my perfect weekend with no sign of Rocco. My father seemed a little distracted, there was a lot of coming and goings, especially late at night. Mid that week I sat at the kitchen table, my father eating a meal, hastily.

"Papa, is everything okay? You seem, well, anxious," I asked.

He did his, waving of the hand, dismissing me, thing. Something was agitating him, that much I was sure of. On two occasions I lifted the telephone to call Rocco, I had never called him at home before and both times I was interrupted. I wasn't, at first, concerned that I hadn't seen him. There had been times over the past months that we might go a week before he would either sneak into my bedroom or arrange for us to meet. I wanted to speak to him to find out what was going on, what had made my father so jumpy.

I managed to catch Jonathan one evening, alone. He had come to get some signatures from father and as I was showing him to the door, I stepped outside.

"Jonathan, what's going on? I haven't seen Rocco at all this week."

"It's okay, Evelyn, Rocco is fine. You know I can't tell you but, please, don't worry. This will all be sorted in a couple of days."

"When you see him, tell him I miss him," I said.

He smiled, hugged me before leaving and getting into the car that had been waiting by the sidewalk. We seemed to have Paulo staying with us and I wondered why. I also noticed the bulge in the side of his jacket. If he was carrying a gun, I was going to be really pissed. There were children in the house.

****

The weekend came with still no sign of Rocco. I was starting to get worried. I knew, sometimes, he would travel for business but Jonathan would have said, wouldn't he? I was being kept in the dark, that much I was aware of. Late one evening, desperate for news, I asked my father where he was.

"Away, *bella*, why do you ask?" he replied.

"Oh, he has my coat in his car, I just wanted to get it back," I stammered.

"Your coat?"

"Yes, he gave me a lift home, a while ago. I left it in his car."

"I'm sure you can get it back when he returns," he said.

So Rocco had been sent somewhere, that would be why he hadn't been in touch, but where? He wouldn't have been able to ring the house, to speak to me, and I wasn't going to get my father to divulge without arousing suspicion. I would wait until I could speak to Jonathan, demand to know where he was.

The following day, I took myself off to work but couldn't concentrate. My mind was on Rocco the whole day. I asked Mr Philips if I could finish a half hour early, I made up a story about a doctor's appointment and headed out to hail a cab. Giving Rocco's address I settled in the back. I wasn't sure whether I was doing the right thing, I had been told he was 'away' but I needed to know. Pulling up outside, I asked the driver to wait for me. I knocked on the door, there was no answer. I stepped to the side and looked through a window. Nothing looked out of place, there was still the washcloth over the arm of the sofa that I had used when I was tidying up and forgot to put back. I climbed back in the cab and gave the address for home. A sadness started to engulf me and I squeezed my eyes shut to stop the tears from falling.

We couldn't get close to the house, cars lined the driveway, people were milling about. Most I recognised, some I didn't. Jonathan paced the drive puffing away at his cigar. I climbed out of the car, knowing someone would mention to my father that I had arrived home in a cab, without caring. As I walked towards the house, as I saw the look on Jonathan's face, I started to run. Something terrible had happened. Was it my father? Joey? Maria? He caught me in his arms before I could barrel through the front door.

"What is it? What's happened?" I asked, panic rising in my voice.

He closed his eyes.

"I'm sorry, Ev..." before he could finish, I pulled away.

"Papa," I shouted.

"No, Ev, your father's fine, he's in the house. It's..."

I looked at him. "No, oh God, no. Please, tell me you're wrong. Please, Jonathan."

Everyone was staring at me but I didn't care. Jonathan held my arm and walked me into the house, into the room my father was sitting with his guys.

"Ev, Rocco had to return to his village, his sister was hurt, an accident or something. He didn't want you to know in case you worried. He was only going for a couple of days and then he would be back, but..." Jonathan trailed off, looking at my father.

"Does someone want to fill me in here? Why are you involving my daughter in this?" I knew my father was angry, he gesticulated with his hands. He only did that when he was mad.

"Evelyn and Rocco have been together, for a while, Joe. They were in love," Jonathan answered.

I turned sharply to him. "Were? We still are."

"Papa, we were going to tell you, he was going to marry me. I've been in love with him my whole life. Where is he?"

The look on my father's face was pure shock. He had not been expecting that at all. A silence fell across the room. No one moved.

"Ev, Rocco was killed, his car was run off the road, we think. We don't know all the details just yet, but I will find out." Jonathan told me.

I heard the words, of course, but they didn't register. I just stood, shaking my head, trying to dislodge them from my ears, from my brain. I heard my father rise from his chair and then I heard a strange noise, an animalistic, guttural, sound. It took a while before I realised the sound was coming from me. I couldn't get my breath, I doubled over in pain before falling to my knees.

"I didn't know. I mean, I knew there was a boy, but not Rocco," I heard my father say as he knelt before me.

He tried to gather me in his arms but I pushed myself away.

"You knew though, papa, you knew he would be killed if he went back and you let him go, you let him go," I said through the sobs.

"*Bella*, how could I stop him? If I'd know about you, you two, I would have. I would have stopped him, you believe that, don't you?"

I looked at him, his eyes beseeching.

"Why didn't I know, Evelyn, why?" he said, quietly.

'He was too scared to tell you, papa, I was too scared to tell you. This fucking life we lead, we are never free."

I saw feet move, I saw Jonathan usher everyone from the room and close the door gently behind them. I hugged myself, the tears soaking into my lap, droplets of anguish spilling onto the wooden floor. I hurt, my stomach hurt, my legs and arms and head hurt, but most of all, my heart shattered into tiny pieces inside me.

The door to the office opened, a bare set of feet came into view as Maria crouched beside me. She placed her arms around my body and rested her head on my back. She didn't speak, she didn't need to. She rocked me, gently.

"You should have told me. I asked you to find out who it was, you should have said," I heard my father say, angrily, he was looking at Jonathan.

"Papa, I asked Jonathan to keep my secret, until we were ready to tell you," I said through my sobs.

My father knelt down beside me, pulling me into his arms.

"I didn't know," he whispered to me, over and over. I reached out and took his hand in mine and we mourned for a man we had loved.

****

I woke up, I didn't know when, it could have been the following day, or the one after. I was in my night gown, I didn't remember getting undressed. I felt hollow, lost. My cheeks were red and chapped from the salty tears that just would not stop, even in sleep I must have cried, my pillow sodden. The door creaked opened and my father entered. He sat on the edge of the bed, nervous. I reached out for him, I climbed on to his lap and let my head rest on his chest. He seemed to have aged overnight. His arms went around my body and he hugged me so tight, just as he'd done when I was little. He stroked my hair, comforting me.

"Tell me about him, about the two of you?" he asked, gently.

Without looking up I told him. I told him how I had fallen in love with Rocco when I was just sixteen. I felt his body stiffen and I reassured him nothing had happened for two years. I told him how much I loved him, how he had loved me back, I knew he had. I apologised over and over for the lies and I asked his forgiveness.

"There is nothing to forgive, Evelyn. I should apologise to you. This life, it's all I know. I just wanted to protect you, your sister and Joey. I just wanted to provide, give you everything you wanted and I failed."

"You didn't fail, papa, I should have told you. He was scared you would send him away if you knew. He said you wanted me to marry a doctor, a lawyer, he wasn't good enough for me."

"He made you happy, didn't he?" my father asked. I nodded my head.

"Then he was a good man, good enough."

We sat in silence for a while.

"Will you come downstairs, eat something?" he asked.

"Tomorrow, papa, I can't eat today."

"Okay, bella, but tomorrow I'll cook something nice for you."

"Papa, I need to ask you do something for me," I said, the words catching in my throat.

"Anything, I would do anything for you," he replied.

"Make them pay, papa, make them pay for Rocco."

He looked at me, a sadness crept over his face before he nodded. At twenty years old I had finally embraced my father's way of life.

I crawled back into bed and he left, not before I noticed the tears in his eyes. A half hour or so later, as I was dozing, the door opened again. Maria came in and climbed into the bed next to me, without a word she placed an arm around me and we cuddled and cried together. I cried for Rocco, I cried for his family, for me. I remembered our weekend, playing husband and wife and I cried for the life I would never have with him. I would never love anyone the way I loved Rocco. I had given myself to him, I had become a woman under his touch and he would always have a part of my heart, my soul. I would never be complete again.

****

It was nearly a month later that I returned to work. I wasn't the same person, I wasn't happy but I was coping. I treasured that photograph I had taken of him. Maria had taken the camera and had the pictures developed. She had come to my room and handed it to me. For the first time in months, she spoke.

"He loved you too, I heard him tell Jonathan. You need to get up now, Evelyn, if you don't you'll end up like me, please get up."

It was all I needed to hear. I would still grieve, I would go to the church and pray and I tried my hardest to return to some form of normality. Four weeks to the day, Jonathan handed me a letter. An airmail sticker on the top corner and the postage mark from Italy made my heart stop. I didn't recognise the writing and my hands shook as I held it. I needed to be alone and took myself to the garden. With the sun setting on the horizon, reminding me of those last moments in Rocco's courtyard, I opened it.

Dear Evelyn,

I can't tell you how sad we all are and how much I would have loved to have met you, I still do. My son spoke of you often with such affection. I didn't want him to come here. It broke my heart to send him away, to your family. I didn't know he was coming until he had arrived. It was a silly accident Adriana had been involved in, Rocco panicked. He shouldn't have come. We still don't know for sure what happened, I don't think we will ever know. Your father has friends, they are searching for the other car involved, then we will know. I found this, by his bed. I don't know if he intended to send this or perhaps he was practising what to say when he returned to you, but I thought you should have it.

If you ever can, Evelyn, please visit. I want to know the woman that my son loved so deeply.

Dina xxx

I held in my hand another piece of paper, folded into four. Just a plain white, scrap piece of paper with torn edges. It looked as if it had been folded and unfolded many times, creases divided up the page. I stared at it for a long time.

I didn't tell you, but I do love you, Evelyn, and I will tell you every day and more. I don't know why I am writing this, I don't think I will ever give it you, I'm just writing my thoughts, preparing for when I see you next. I want it all straight in my head when I ask your father for his blessing, to marry you. I picture that day, you will be beautiful and you will be mine. I'll be the proudest man, watching you walk on your father's arm, to be handed over to me.

I'm sitting here, among the olive trees imagining you here, our children playing in the grass. This is something that will always just be a dream though. Perhaps, later, who knows. I want a daughter, Evelyn. I want a daughter who will look just like you, then a son and I will cherish them. I'll work hard, we can start our own business, a safe one and buy a house. I want that life so much, it hurts.

You gave me the ultimate gift, yourself. I hear your moans in my head, when my hands touch you and all I want to do is lie next to you, holding you in my arms. I want to feel your skin, so smooth, so soft. I want to stroke your hair and kiss your lips. I want, well, you know what I want.

I'll be home tomorrow and the first thing I'm going to do is find you. I don't care who knows, I love you. I want everyone to know that. I LOVE YOU.

There was no signature, it wasn't a letter as such, more a jumble of thoughts and a note to himself. I held it to my chest, it would become, along with the photograph my most treasured possession. Something that would go to the grave with me. I didn't need possessions, I didn't need fancy shoes or rings, I just needed confirmation that I had been right. This man had loved me and that one year we had together would be enough to last me a lifetime. I would never love another man the same, I would never completely give my heart, for me, there would only ever be Rocco.

****

I wasn't paying attention, I was fumbling in my bag for a cigarette, something to calm the sickness inside when I felt a tug on the strap. I looked up and into the black eyes of a... Well, I wasn't quite sure of his age. He was as tall as me, broad shoulders but a child's face, a dirty face. I watched as he ran holding my purse, the purse that contained the only picture I had of Rocco. A sadness engulfed me and my knees buckled. I found myself kneeling on the cold, dirty sidewalk and not one person came to my aid. I bowed my head and I let the tears flow. I felt no embarrassment just an overwhelming sense of sadness. I thought that I would never again be able to hold that photo to my heart, to whisper words of love to it in dark, lonely nights.

A shadow fell across my lap and I looked up as the boy crouched in front of me. His dark eyes just staring. I moved slightly back, to get a little distance, I wasn't sure of his motive and then he surprised me. He handed me back my purse.

"My friend is sick, I needed some money for medicine," he said.

That was the day that I met Robert Stone, the boy that would save me. The boy that I would care for as if he was my own and who would help me mend my broken heart. The boy who would grow to be a remarkable, powerful, wealthy man, who looked upon my father as his own.

The boy who gave me a reason to continue to live.

Dear Reader,

We all have moments in our lives that we treasure, memories that, as we get older, fade but can always be called upon when we need them, for comfort. That one weekend with Rocco is mine. Over the years that followed, I've often thought of Rocco and what could have been. That old saying rings so true - to have loved and lost is better than to have never loved at all.

I wrote to Dina for many years, I was saddened never to have met her and even sadder to hear of her passing. Adriana and I, to this day, still exchange letters. They have a comfortable life, it appears Rocco had provided for his family, financially, although I suspect my father may have had a hand in that. I'm hoping to visit soon, to meet her family and her son, named after his uncle. I've had plenty of opportunity to visit Italy in the past but never been able to bring myself to go. It was only when I received an airline ticket, for a family holiday one Christmas, that I knew, now was the right time. With my family beside me, I would go. I would visit Rocco's grave and I would love him all over again.

Don't waste a moment, don't waste an opportunity to tell that special person you love them. Don't spend your life mourning or wishing for something better. You only have one life, make it count, live it to the fullest.

I never really fell in love again. It wasn't because I couldn't have, that I felt I would betray Rocco. I just never found another who could make me feel the way Rocco did. I love my family and that's enough for me.

This isn't the happy ending I would have loved, but had my life not taken the path it did, I would never have been on that street that day. I would never have shed tears that made a young boy come back to me. Fate brought Robert and Travis into my life, or maybe Rocco did, who knows. Whatever it was, I am truly thankful.

Evelyn

An introduction to the next installment in the Fallen Angel series ~ Robert

Chapter one from the next installment of the

Fallen Angel Series

Robert

This book can be read as a prequel to Fallen Angel, Part I and is his story, his life, told in his words.

(Subject to change prior to publication)

Chapter 1

The house was empty when I arrived home from school. I fished out the key attached by a piece of string to the inside of my blazer pocket. I wasn't surprised to find myself alone, it was quite normal. I shrugged off my blazer and unclipped the red striped tie we were made to wear, hanging them neatly on the banister. I made my way to the kitchen, dropped my bag on the floor and opened the fridge. There was a piece of cheese as hard as a brick, a half empty tin of beans and a carton of milk. I sniffed the milk. I had learnt over the years that if it had a certain smell it wouldn't taste nice. It seemed fine so I poured it over some slightly soft cereal in a bowl. I switched on the TV and waited. They never came home.

I must have fallen asleep on the sofa and it was dark outside when I was awoken by a knock at the front door. The room was illuminated only by the flickering screen of the TV. I waited until there was a second knock before I made my way to the hall. I wasn't normally allowed to open the door, but maybe it was them. Maybe they had forgotten their door key.

I looked through the letter box, someone outside bent down so their eyes were level with mine.

"Hello son, can you open the door for us?" he asked.

He looked like a policeman, I had seen them before. They came to my school sometimes and of course I had seen them on the TV.

"My mum says I'm not allowed to open the door, to anyone," I said.

"Is there an adult with you? Can they open the door?" he asked.

"No," I replied, quietly.

I watched the man stand up, speak to someone behind him before crouching back down again.

"It's okay son, we just need to come in and make sure you're all right," he said.

"I had my tea," I replied. "I made it myself."

"Well, that's good, what did you have?"

"Cornflakes," I said. "I like cornflakes."

"I like cornflakes too," he replied. "Did you have lots of milk?"

That was silly, of course I had lots of milk, everyone has lots of milk with cornflakes, don't they? He stood again and then I saw Nora from next door, she placed her hand on the letterbox, her old creaky legs bent down so she could see through.

"Robert, can you open the door, love," she said.

I liked Nora, she gave me sweets sometimes. She would be in the garden pegging out her washing and she would see me peering over the fence at her. Smiling, she would raise her fingers to her lips, creep back into her house and come out with a packet of boiled sweets. Sometimes they were so sticky I couldn't get the wrapper off. I wasn't allowed sweets normally, bad for your teeth and full of animal stuff, my mum used to tell me.

I opened the door and outside, standing under the little porch light was Nora and the policeman, there was another coming up the path, a police lady. I stood, blocking the way.

"Can we come in son?" the man asked.

At school my teacher had told me that we should always listen and be polite to the police so I let them pass and followed into the lounge. Nora crouched down to my level.

"Robert, is there anyone here with you?" she asked.

"No, I'm waiting for my mum and dad. They're normally home by now," I said, shaking a little.

Something was wrong, I could sense it. I had seen the look that passed between the police and Nora just before she ushered me to the sofa and sat next to me. She took my hand in hers and it felt odd. I don't think anyone had held my hand before. My mum pulled me across the road sometimes by it, if I wasn't quick enough. I looked at my hand in hers. She had funny, bent fingers and long, yellowing nails. It looked like she had been gardening again, she had dirty fingertips.

"Robert, have you got any aunties, someone who lives near by?" she asked.

I shook my head, I didn't think so. My mum would talk on the phone to people but no one ever visited us. Unless my dad was around, she never really left the house either.

"What about nanny, where does she live?" she asked.

I thought for a minute. "I don't think I have one of them."

"Son, how old are you?" the man asked.

"Six, I will be seven in two months and twenty-eight days," I replied, proudly. I was good at math.

"Your mum didn't leave anyone here to look after you?" He asked.

"No, I come home from school and sometimes they're out so I make my own tea. I have reading to do, I can read well now."

I picked up my school book to show them. It was one I had selected from the bookshelf in my class about football, but they didn't seem interested. Nora stood, they huddled together whispering and I watched them, trying real hard to hear what was being said.

"Where's my mum?" I asked, hating that my voice quivered a little.

I was trying to be strong, that's what my mum would have wanted. She hated it if I cried, she would want me to be strong, "Be a man" she would say. I tried to be a man.

"I have some terrible news, Robert," Nora said to me, as she sat back down. "Your mum and dad, well, there's been an accident, in the car."

"Are they in the hospital?" I asked.

"Well, yes they are, but..."

"Can I go and see them?" I interrupted.

"Robert, the thing is, no you can't see them. Oh love, they..., they've gone to heaven," Nora blurted out, her face screwed up in sadness.

"Heaven," the voice in my head said. "I doubt that very much."

I didn't have voices in my head all the time, not like mad people got. Just every now and again a voice would warn me of something, like to look further up the road and when I did there would be a bike coming that I hadn't noticed before. My mum said I have good instinct. I didn't know what that meant, but right then I hoped it was a good thing.

The policeman and Nora were chatting, the police lady came and sat on the other side of me, she seemed friendly and she smiled at me.

"Do you have any friends, Robert, maybe someone you stayed overnight with?" she asked.

I shook my head, my mum didn't really like me to have friends. I was never allowed to bring anyone home.

"No aunties, uncles?"

"My dad used to speak to someone, she lives in a different country. I think it was his sister," I volunteered. "I answered the phone once, she said Happy Easter to me."

"Do you know her name or maybe she had an accent, did she sound funny?" she asked.

"Yes, my teacher has the same voice," I replied, excited. "He comes from America. I saw America on a map once, shall I show it to you?"

I had a map book in my bedroom. My dad used to sit on my bed and talk about all the different countries. He would make up a story about a little boy who would travel the world. I knew it was made up because he called the little boy Robert and I hadn't been anywhere. Running up the stairs, I pulled down the book from the shelf above my bed.

I showed the policeman the book, smiling because I found America straight away. He patted me on the head before he made his way to the front door speaking on the black thing he had attached to his jacket.

****

That night I stayed with Nora, she had a little back bedroom, same as mine and she tucked me into bed. Sitting on the edge, she watched me and stroked my black hair away from my forehead.

"So, if they have gone to heaven, does that mean they're not coming back?" I asked.

"Oh love, no, they're not coming back," she said.

"Where am I going to live?"

"Let's worry about that tomorrow, shall we?" she replied.

She sat with me for a while. She didn't have to, I thought, but it was nice to have someone stroke my hair. As I lay in the dark, I thought about my mum and dad and what Nora had told me. Maybe I should be crying but however much I screwed my eyes shut, the tears wouldn't come. I pinched myself on the arm, hard enough to bruise, but that didn't make me cry either. I felt something strange in my belly though, like a pain but not a pain, it was like my belly was empty. Maybe I just needed something to eat.

Downstairs Nora met with the police again and this time someone new, I could hear them chatting. I heard the word Social Services but I didn't know what that meant. I crept to the top of the stairs and listened. They were saying that I would stay with Nora until emergency foster parents could be found in the morning. I would have liked to have stayed at home, I was okay on my own. I knew how to make my tea, I did it all the time and I didn't want to miss school. I liked school.

The following morning a new lady came, she said her name was Sarah, she was going to take me to her house to stay for a while. She told me about the toys she had there, that I could play with. She was an older woman but she had kind eyes. I liked people's eyes, it told me a lot about them. I could always tell if someone was friendly or not by their eyes. My mum asked me about it once. She wanted to know how I knew what people were like just by looking at them. I couldn't answer the question though, I thought everybody could see what I saw. I got told off a lot for staring though.

"Are you ready?" Sarah asked as we stood in the sitting room.

"I think so. Can I get my teddy?" I asked.

She looked at Nora. "Do you have a key?" She asked.

"I don't, maybe the police do," Nora answered.

Sarah bent down to my level, she looked straight at me with a smile.

"How about I get in touch with someone later and we can ask," she said.

She took me in a car; I sat in the back and we drove, not very far, until we pulled into her driveway. She had a small house in a little lane with fields either side and a dog. It came bounding to the door when she opened it. It was only little but licked my face when I bent down to stroke it's rough brown fur. I liked her dog, she told me he was called Benny. Benny and me became friends, we played in the garden and I stayed at Sarah's house for a few weeks.

****

I liked the house, it was bigger than mine and there were lots of windows. At home, my mum used to pull the curtains closed all the time, making the rooms dark, but at Sarah's it was always light. I had a bedroom to myself, there were no other children but some must have lived there before because there were so many boxes of toys and not just for boys either. I found a box of dolls which I put straight back under the bed.

"Sarah, there are dolls under the bed," I told her.

"I know, I don't suppose you want to play with them. Would you like me to put them somewhere else?" She replied.

"No, it's okay, I just wanted you to know."

"Your tea will be ready soon, do you want to go and wash your hands?" she said.

One of the best things was that Sarah cooked proper food. I found it strange to sit at a dining table and eat with a knife and fork, I had forgotten how to use them. At school I had sandwiches for lunch and at home we usually ate something in a bowl with a spoon. It was at tea time that Sarah and me talked. We would talk about all sorts of things, school, my mum and dad and sometimes she asked me how I felt but I didn't know the words, so I said nothing about that. At night she would tuck me in bed and sit with me, either to read or just to put her arm around my shoulders. My mum wasn't a huggy person so it was good to snuggle up to Sarah sometimes, not always, but just sometimes when I was scared. She always smelled lovely and I liked to bury my head in her shoulder and listen to her voice as she read to me. She read me a book about another little boy who had lost his mum and dad. But this little boy used to cry and I wondered why I didn't. Then I would remember, I was being a man and men don't cry - I know that because my mum told me, men don't cry.

I did go back to school after a couple of days and people were different to me. The teachers a bit kinder. Not that they were horrible in the first place but the kids were strange around me, as if they didn't want to be friends anymore. It was not like I had many friends at school. I was more interested in learning new things than chatting, but at playtime I might be invited to play football or climb on the frame. They didn't ask me anymore, but I saw them whisper about me, behind their hands, their eyes looking my way. I wanted to ask them what they were talking about but I never did, I just sat on my own until playtime was over.

****

One day I was taken to the Head Masters office, there was a man there that I didn't know and I hoped I was not in trouble. I was asked to sit down as the man wanted to have a chat to me.

"Hello, Robert, my name is David, I'm a doctor," he said.

"Hello," I replied. I wasn't sick, well, I didn't think I was.

"I thought it might be good to have a chat, maybe about your mum and dad."

"Oh, okay," I replied.

"Do you want to talk about them?" he asked.

Did I? Sarah asked me many questions about them and I didn't mind talking to her but I didn't know this man and my mum told me not to talk to strangers.

"Not really," I said.

He asked me if I felt sad about them dying. What a dumb question, of course I was sad. They were dead. I didn't answer so he asked me if I liked being at Sarah's house.

"I like Benny," I said. "Sarah is nice, she cooks real food you know. She made me, oh what was it called, spaghetti something last night. I've never had that before, I think it comes from abroad. We got real messy when we ate, it was fun."

"Did your mum ever cook?" he asked.

I shook my head. No, my mum rarely cooked, we lived on whatever could be opened and eaten straight away. Sometimes there was no real food in the house so we just had toast or cereal. I had heard my dad shout at her once, about making sure I had a proper meal each night but it never happened. I had my main meal at school, at lunchtimes. It was usually a little packed lunch that came in a bag, a sandwich and a piece of fruit. If the dinner lady was feeling really kind, she would give me a bar of chocolate.

"What about your dad?" he asked. "Do you want to talk about him?"

"My dad didn't live with us all the time," I said.

Sometimes he would, he would stay for a few days but then got the calling, as my mum would put it. He wanted to be an artist, he used to draw pictures of me and I had them pinned to the wall in my bedroom. Sometimes he had to go, sort his head out, I was told. I guessed everyone's dad did that. I missed him when he was gone. My mum was always sad then. Sometimes she would shout and scream about his other family, I didn't know what she meant. She would point to me and tell me I had made him go away and that he didn't love us enough to stay.

It was at times like that I did what I knew made her happy. I poured the brown stuff from the bottle under the sink and she would cry while she drank lots of it. After a while she would fall asleep on the sofa and I would cover her over with a blanket. She would still be there in the morning, looking really strange. She would have little lines of black paint running down her cheeks from her eyelashes. I would try to rub it away with my fingers sometimes, to make her pretty again. I hated the smell of the brown stuff. One day I had tasted it. It was like drinking fire, it burnt my mouth and my throat. It made me cough and my eyes watered.

"Do you think your mum loved you?" he asked, now this startled me.

After thinking for a moment, I answered.

"No," I said with clarity.

I knew she didn't love me, I think she liked me though, I was no trouble. I kept myself to myself and stayed in my bedroom most of the time. I did what I was told, I didn't cry and whine like other kids. I dressed and cleaned my teeth without being asked every morning. I took myself off to school when the big hand on the clock said so and I brought myself home straight after. She never hit me, ever.

"Why do you think your mum didn't love you?" He asked.

I didn't answer. When it was home time, other kids had mums that hugged them and laughed and asked them how their day had been. I watched kids show their mum a drawing or a book. Mine never did that and if I showed her a book she would swipe her arm, knocking it to the floor. She told me not to fill my head with rubbish. I didn't know how to fill my head with rubbish but I liked reading my books. If she loved me, she would laugh and be happy, wouldn't she?

Session over, I went back to my class with no real understanding of what that was all about.

So it went on, people asking me questions about my parents and how did I feel about it? Throughout the whole time I had not shed one tear. I didn't think they would understand what was going on in my head, so I said very little. I didn't like them keep asking questions, especially when I did answer them. I started to get angry.

"Did your mum ever hit you?"

"No."

"Did your mum ever hug you?"

"No."

"Did your mum play with you?"

"No."

"Did your dad play with you?"

"Sometimes."

I saw the way their eyes shifted, the way their eyebrows went up when I answered. I was not stupid, they didn't like my mum or maybe they didn't believe me. The more they asked, the more confused and quieter I became. The stiller I was, the more nervous they became, they seemed uncomfortable around me. I felt it, I saw it in their eyes.

****

A few weeks had passed and after returning from school one day, I met an elderly woman. Apparently she was my aunt Edith, my dad's sister and the person I had spoken to on the phone that one time. She looked so different to me. She had grey hair, pulled back in a tight bun and runny, grey eyes with fair, leathery skin. Then again, my mum and dad looked different too. I had black hair and dark, dark eyes. Sometimes I would look in the mirror and I couldn't decide if they were brown or black. My mum was blonde with light hazel eyes and as much as I tried, I couldn't quite remember what colour my dad's eyes were. I got upset when I couldn't remember the colour, I didn't want to forget him.

"Robert, this is Edith, she's your aunt and she's come from America to visit you," Sarah said.

"Hello, Robert, I'm pleased to finally meet you," Edith replied, holding out her hand for me to shake.

I wasn't sure what to do, but I shook it anyway.

"Hello," I replied.

"I'm sorry to hear about your mum and dad. I've been asked to take you home, with me for a while," she said.

I didn't want to go, I was happy at Sarah's but what I didn't like the most was that she didn't have kind eyes. She never looked at me, she never let me look at her. If I tried to move my head, to look at her face, she would turn away slightly. It confused me.

"Thank you but I don't want to," I replied.

"I have a house with a woods and guess what? Some deer come and feed in the garden," Edith said.

Deer? That made me smile. I had never seen a real one before.

"Wow, that sounds cool," I said, getting a little excited.

Sarah sat beside me and sometimes I caught them looking at each other, over my head. Sarah would nod and smile at Edith but her smile didn't seem right. It wasn't the same smile she would give me. The smile that made the skin around her eyes crinkle. She didn't like Edith, I thought, and I wondered why. You see, if the skin around the eyes crinkled it was a good smile, a friendly one. If it didn't, then I knew it wasn't good. That was one of the reasons I liked to look at people's eyes.

"There's a school nearby you can go to, but you have get a bus. It will pick you up at the top of the lane every morning. I spoke with the school, they are looking forward to meeting you," Edith said.

"Oh, what about my own school?" I asked.

"They won't mind, as long as you go to school it doesn't matter which one it is, does it Sarah," she replied.

Sarah never answered but kept that strange half smile on her face. Edith was to collect me a couple of days later I was told. After she had left Sarah and me sat in the sitting room. She seemed a bit sad and I took her hand.

"It's okay, Sarah. I won't be gone long and we can take Benny to the park when I get back," I said.

She smiled sadly at me, patted my hand and went to make dinner. I did notice she had tears in her eyes though.

I wanted to go back to my old house to collect some things. Driving past it one day, on the way to school, I had noticed a sign outside, it had been put up for sale. I didn't know who was dealing with that, I guess my aunt would, but then, what did I know about these things. It seemed my aunt thought that the best thing was to forget about my parents as soon as possible. She never mentioned them and I knew that she hadn't seen her brother for many years. We have lived in the same house all my life and she had never visited. She only ever rang at Easter and Christmas to speak to my dad. Not that he was there every Christmas. When he wasn't I didn't get a present, we didn't have a cooked meal or laugh and have fun. It was just a normal day.

She had told me we were going on a plane to America. At first I had thought it was a holiday, I would be back. I didn't have time to say goodbye to anyone, I would have liked to have said goodbye to my teacher at least. I would've also liked to have taken some of my own clothes with me and my teddy, the one present my mum ever gave me, but no. We simply got into a car and was driven to the airport. I didn't understand why Sarah was so upset

103

when we climbed into that car, she tried to smile but as she hugged me to her I heard a little sob.

I was excited though, I'd never been on a plane before and with my nose pressed to the window in the departure lounge, I watched them take off and arrive. I bounced around in excitement, wanting to get on that plane quickly, to have an adventure.

The journey was long. I had a window seat and I watched the ground fall away, the clouds disperse as we flew through them until all that was above us was miles and miles of sky. As the night fell, I looked at the stars, so bright and clear. If heaven was above me, then I wondered, if I looked hard enough, could I see my mum and dad? Were they one of the stars that twinkled down at me? Nora had said they had gone to heaven and as she was so old, she must know these things.

I had fallen asleep and was woken by a jolt as the plane landed. The captain announced our arrival in Pittsburgh and after a little while we made our way through the airport. We had no luggage to collect and soon enough we were outside in the sun. The heat was quite something. I had to shield my eyes from the glare of the sun as it reflected off the cars, off the buildings. It smelt different too, the air, I mean.

It felt like a long journey in a cab until eventually we reached the town of Sterling. I read the little sign as a few houses came into view. It was rural with wooden houses dotted around, the complete opposite to where I had lived in a little terrace house in the South East of London. Everyone had a big car, a truck Edith had called them. Some were broken and one we had passed had no wheels. It didn't look very tidy, people had really long grass in the front garden but every now and again, I would spot a kid, playing. They would stop and look at my face pressed to the car window as we passed.

Pulling up at my aunt's house was an eye opener. There were indeed acres of garden and the house was surrounded by woodland. It was one storey but with a basement and a wooden porch wrapping around it. The paint was peeling off the wood and I had to be careful not to tread on the rotted planks. There was a swing seat on the porch and I wanted to sit and throw my legs back and forth to make it rock. I bet it even made a creaking sound too.

Aunt Edith showed me to my new bedroom. It was okay, it had a small metal bed under the one window with a patchwork quilt thrown over it. There was a book shelf, I liked to read, but making my way over to it, I noticed all it held were bibles, all sorts. Some had pictures, some just words. I had seen bibles in school, we had started to learn about the different Gods. There were no colouring books though and I wanted to practice my colouring. I was getting good at keeping the pen inside the lines.

A small wooden wardrobe, which held a collection of clothes for me and a desk with a metal chair were the only other things in the room. No toys, no TV, no books or colouring pens, no teddies, none of the things I had got used to having at Sarah's. There was nothing from my old home, none of the pictures I had on the wall that my dad had drawn. The walls were just bare, painted a sickly yellow colour and there were no curtains at the window. I climbed on the bed to look out the window, all I could see were trees and more trees.

"Do you like your room?" Edith asked. "I got some clothes from the Church, you'll need to thank them. I'm sure they will fit okay."

"Erm, yes, it's nice," I replied. I wasn't sure what she would say if I said no.

"Well, feel free to have a look around," she said, as she made her way out of the room.

While Edith unpacked her small case in the second bedroom, I investigated the rest of the house. I found a kitchen with a wooden, scrubbed table in the middle and mismatched chairs tucked in around it, a lounge with an open fireplace and a couple of battered sofas facing it. In one corner there was a desk with yet more bibles stacked on top and through the kitchen, I found two doors. One led to the bathroom and one to a basement. Down a flight of stairs, I noticed some kind of workbench, stacks and stacks of logs for the fire drying out, piles of old newspapers and tins of paint but that was all.

****

For the first couple of days I was allowed to explore a little, to find my way through the woods and back to the house. I made a plan of camps I could make in there, playing soldiers. Then, on the third day, dressed in shorts and a blue button down shirt, I was sent to school. I had a sandwich and an apple in my back pack and Edith waited at the end of the lane for the bus to arrive. I wasn't scared about going to school on my own, I did it all the time but what bothered me was, if I was on holiday, why did I need to go to school at all?

My mum took me out of school all the time. Sometimes we would drive for long hours to meet my dad who had holed himself up in a beach shack somewhere, to paint. I had not had to go to school though, this was something new.

I climbed aboard the bus, it was nearly full but the kids quietened when I got on so I took the first seat available, next to a girl. She smiled at me. She reminded me a little of my mum, she had blond hair in pigtails and kind, hazel eyes. The first thing I noticed were the bruises on her skinny, bare arms.

"Hi, my name's Cara, what's yours?"

"Robert," was all I said, shyly.

"You speak funny," she said, but I didn't think she was being unkind.

"Well, so do you. I come from England," I replied.

"Where's that?"

I shrugged my shoulders. "I had to get on a plane so it must have been far away."

"I've never been on a plane before," she said.

"It was cool, really fast and we went really high in the sky. I could see the stars and everything," I gushed.

"You saw the stars? I love looking at the stars, they're so pretty," she said, excitedly.

We arrived at the school, there was a woman waiting to meet us and I was escorted off the bus with Cara in tow and led to a classroom. I was introduced to my new teacher, Father Peters and I didn't like him, he didn't have friendly eyes at all. I sat next to Cara that day, she showed me where we went to eat our lunch and she was kind to me. My first ever friend, I thought. The school was small, attached to the church and when it was play time there were no swings, no climbing frame, none of the things I had back home. Cara and I sat on the dried up grass and just chatted.

Tracie Podger

"Where do you live?" I asked.

"Not too far, we have a farm."

"That's cool, do you have animals?"

"Yes, I have to get up early and feed the chickens every day, they run around the yard and sometimes get in the house," she said, with a laugh.

"Can I come and see them one day?" I asked.

"Erm, well, my dad is not real friendly. I don't think he would like that," she replied.

"Oh, is your mum friendly?" I asked.

"Yes, when she's not sad."

"My mum was always sad, she's dead you know. So is my dad."

"Oh, that's real terrible. Who do you live with?"

"My aunt, her name is Edith. Do you have any brothers?" I asked.

"I had a sister but she doesn't live with us anymore. I miss her."

"Oh. I don't have any brothers or sisters, it's just me," I replied.

At the end of the day we travelled back on the bus together and she got off long before me. None of the other kids spoke to me although they whispered a lot behind their hands, their eyes looking my way, but I just ignored them.

When the bus stopped at the top of the lane to Edith's house there was no one to greet me. Some of the other kids had mums or dads at their stop who bundled them up into a hug. I just made my way down the lane to the house. Edith was always there, she left the house only once a day, every day, to go to church and then once a week to the grocery store. Why someone would want to go to church every day was beyond me, I'd never been to a church before.

Edith had a list of things I had to do, she had written them down on a large piece of paper that she pinned up on the kitchen wall. It would change from day to day but some of the things remained the same. I had to sweep the front yard, start repainting the wooden rails around the porch and make sure there were enough logs cut and stacked for winter. Sawing logs was a new one to me, I would find the fallen branches in the woods and drag them until sweat dripped off my brow, all the way back to the house.

Then I would saw them into smaller pieces until blisters formed on my hands. Lastly, and luckily, she had a splitter. The logs had to be exactly the same size, ready for storing for the fire or the stove, or she would make me do them again. It never dawned on me that someone of my age should not be doing these things. I would have to help sweep the house as there were no carpets anywhere, the occasional rug but otherwise it was just wooden floors throughout. I would then clean the kitchen, wash the dishes each night and finally, exhausted, I did my homework and fell into bed. I didn't mind being busy, it kept me warm. Even in the summer the house was always chilly and Edith wouldn't have the fire going. The warmest place was either, fully clothed under my quilt or in front of the stove.

Edith and I never really spoke much, she never asked me about my day, what I had done at school. She would sit at her desk each night and read from her bible, aloud. I would sit and listen, there was not much else I could do really. She didn't have a TV to watch and other than my school book, I had nothing to read. Sometimes she would read then ask me questions, if I couldn't answer she would get cross. She would squint her eyes at me, tut and read the passage again, slower.

****

The first time she beat me was about a month after I had arrived. It was when I was late home from school. The bus had a flat so we didn't leave at our usual time. By the time I had arrived home, I was fifteen minutes late. Edith was at the end of the lane, at the stop waiting for me. I smiled when we arrived, it was unusual but good to see her. My smile soon faded when I saw the look in her eyes, she meant me harm, I could tell.

She dragged me by the arm from the bus in front of everyone, her fingers dug into my skin and my face burnt with embarrassment. She pushed me in front of her, forcing me to march the path to the house and then I heard it, a whoosh, followed by a sting across my back. The buckle end of a belt bit into my skin. I turned in shock, no one had ever hit me before and she lashed out again, catching my side, then my stomach.

"I know what you are, what you are up to," she screamed at me, repeatedly.

As quick as I stumbled backwards, she came forwards, swinging her arm, the belt wrapped around her hand and the end catching any part of my body it could. She was cursing me but I didn't understand what she was saying.

This could not be because I was late, it was not my fault after all.

I held my hands over the areas she had already hit, trying to take away the pain and ran to the house. When I got on with my chores she stopped but she took up her bible and starting reading aloud to me, following me from room to room. I didn't cry, in hindsight, I didn't have the ability to. I guessed I must have cried as a baby but my mum hated it if I cried and soon enough I learnt not to.

I went to bed that day without any dinner, hungry and confused. What had I done that had deserved that beating? As I lay on my bed the only comfort I got were my thoughts of a previous life, back in England. Whether my mum and dad were good or bad, whether they left me alone or not, it was better than where I was.

The following morning as I dressed I noticed a clear liquid weeping from the cut on my side. I tried to wipe it with tissue but it stung. I pulled on my school shirt and watched it darken as the liquid soaked into it. My back hurt, my body was stiff and it was an effort to walk up the lane to catch the bus. Every step I took made the shirt rub against my wounds.

I took my seat, quietly, next to Cara.

"Are you okay?" she asked.

I just nodded. I was too embarrassed to say anything. We got through the morning, although I fidgeted on my chair and the Father was constantly yelling at me to sit still. At lunch time, Cara pulled at the back of my shirt. I winced, the shirt had stuck to my cuts and as it pulled away, one had started to bleed. She held the back of my shirt and just looked at me for a while.

"Come with me," she said.

We snuck back into the school, into the toilet where she wet some tissue and wiped my side. The cold water was soothing. We didn't speak but I knew she understood what had happened.

"It stops hurting after a while," she said, as we left for class.

I can't say the beatings were a daily thing but it seemed that at least every other day there would be a problem and I would take the punishment for it. Sometimes she would come back from church and beat me for no reason. She started to make me sit at her feet and she would preach the bible at me, with one hand on my forehead. What she was doing, I had no idea.

"Submit yourself therefore to God. Resist the devil, and he will flee from you," she would say.

She would close her eyes and rock back and forth, her hand never leaving my forehead as she seemed to be chanting. Sometimes I couldn't hear, she would mumble and other times she would shout out loud. The same thing, repeatedly. I didn't know what her words meant. She talked about the devil a lot.

My life consisted of going to school and coming back to the house, I would never refer to it as home, being beaten and if not beaten then being preached to. At one point Edith had grabbed me by the shoulders, forced me to my knees in front of her and announced that I was the devil. She wanted to help me, to get the devil out of me, make me pure. She told me that my parents were dead because of me, because I had the devil inside. When she said those things my hands would shake with fear. I wasn't sure what I was scared of though, being the devil or her.

****

Cara and I became best friends. She would help me up from my chair when the bruises and the welts from the belt stung on the back of my legs and made me stiff. She would pick leaves from a prickly plant, slice them open and make me rub the sticky, smelly stuff inside, on my cuts. I would do the same for her. Every day that I went to school in pain, so did she. We only ever had one conversation about it.

"Who does this to you?" I had asked her one day.

She had a bruise on her cheek, the skin grazed and when she sat and her skirt raised, I could see bruising on her thighs. I wasn't trying to look at her legs but the marks looked just like handprints. She had tried to pull her skirt down when she noticed me looking.

"My dad," she whispered. "He does things to me but you mustn't tell anyone, promise me."

"What does he do?" I asked.

"He touches me, down there, and hits me if I cry." She pointed between her thighs.

"He's not allowed to do that though," I said.

She just shrugged her shoulders.

"Don't you tell your mum?" I asked.

"I did once, he told her I was a dirty little liar and then he killed my cat. He drowned her in the water butt, she had babies and I tried to help them but they needed their momma's milk."

Her eyes filled with tears at the memory. We linked our little fingers and made a promise to each other that we wouldn't tell, because, I guessed, we knew if we did, things would get worse.

It was at this time that I started to feel hatred. For Cara's dad, for my aunt, for my parents, for my teacher, for everyone. The only time this boiling inside me ceased was when I was with Cara, she make me feel calm. Even at the age I was then I knew what was happening to her and I felt angry that I was too young and powerless to stop it.

****

I had been with Edith for just under a couple of years and I hated her, and where I was, with every fibre of my being. Every time I looked at her, I would get a taste in my mouth, like after I had been sick, and I would have to swallow hard to get rid of it. I knew then that was what hatred tasted like.

"Are you the devil?" I would ask myself as I looked in the cracked mirror in the bathroom.

The face that stared back at me, the black eyes, for a while was unsure. If Edith was so sure, she must be right. She was a church goer, so she must know what she was talking about. For a while, I willingly sat at her feet, I didn't want to be the devil. I would let her beat me, berate and cleanse me until I was pure again. However, there were times when I hoped she was right. If I was the devil I might have special powers to make this stop. I might have special powers to stop what was happening to Cara. Somewhere inside me I had this feeling of really wanting to hurt Edith, the way she hurt me, but I never did. I would dream of putting my hands around her scrawny neck and squeezing until she couldn't breathe. I could picture her face, the fear in her bulging eyes. I could feel her hands on mine trying to pull them away, her dirty nails scraping my skin and I could smell death as she took her last breath.

I wanted her to feel how I did inside, the sadness, the pain and the confusion. I wanted her to feel the ache in my stomach that would never go away and I wanted her to feel the loneliness I felt. I began to hate school as well which did upset me. People kept their distance, but they whispered about me.

"Why don't they talk to me?" I asked one time, looking around the lunch hall.

"Because they're scared of you," Cara said, quite matter of fact.

"You talk to me though."

"Because, silly, you don't scare me," she replied.

"I don't mean to scare people, what are they scared of?"

"Your eyes, you have the black eyes, that's what scares them. You like, stare at people."

Well, I couldn't help the colour of my eyes, could I. I can't help if I stare at people, I am only trying to see if I can work out what they are thinking, that's all.

****

As fall turned into winter, the beatings got worse. It seemed to be my fault the plumbing froze or the stove didn't work, I had cursed this house she would scream at me. It was my fault the newly painted porch made the rest of the house look shabby. It was my fault the logs were too big and they didn't stack well enough. However, as she, and I, got older, I got wiser. I managed to hide from her for a while, I had my camp in the woods, somewhere she couldn't find me.

I would come home from school, quickly do my chores and head out to the woods. I liked being outdoors, if I could, I would live there forever. It was peaceful, it was clean and it was exactly as it should be. I had spent the whole summer making my camp. I nailed wood to the trees and covered it with an old tarpaulin I had found. It was quiet and peaceful. If Cara managed to get out after school, she would meet me there. We would sit and plan our escape. We would talk about imaginary places where we would live together. How we would stow away on a plane and I would take her back to Sarah's. I told her all about Benny and that we could take him for walks in the park. She would love being at Sarah's. I would even let her bring that box of dolls out from under the bed.

"Do you speak to Sarah?" Cara had asked me one time.

"No, I don't know if she knows where I am. I would like to though, I miss her."

I would have loved to have asked my aunt if I could call Sarah but, somehow, I knew she wouldn't allow it. There was never any mention of my life in England, it was if it hadn't existed.

Time after time Cara and I talked about running away. I knew we could do it but she was too scared to try. I would spend hours trying to convince her I would take care of her. I would never beat her, I would hunt to make sure we had food, we could live in the woods forever. I made bows and arrows, I sharpened stones until they could prick my skin, like a knife. I made a pillow for her out of leaves and dried grass that, when she was really sad, she would lay her head on and close her eyes. As she rested her body, I carved our initials into a tree trunk, a symbol that we would be friends forever. I would watch her, that anger boiling away under the surface at what had happened to her. I was only nine years old.

I would sleep outdoors some nights, wrapped up in a blanket I had stolen from the house and watch the night sky, the stars, cursing my parents for being dead and leaving me in his hell hole. Sometimes my chest would hurt with the intensity of it all. I wanted to feel something else, anything, and even when I punched the tree trunk over and over and watched my knuckles bleed, I felt no pain, nothing but this emptiness inside. It was like I was hollow and if I beat my chest it echoed.

What I liked most about being outdoors was that it was constant. The leaves fell at the same time of the year, the flowers opened when they should. I had a sense of time, of purpose when I stayed outside. Inside the house, it was too unpredictable, outside I knew exactly what was going to happen and when.

Some days I would pack my school back pack with food I had stolen. I knew Cara and I could hide away in the woods for however long it took for people to stop looking for us, or so I thought, but we never did. Cara would get upset and cry when I tried to persuade her to run away. I hated to make her cry. Later in life I would often wonder why I stayed for as long as I had, why I endured what I did. But in my heart I knew, I only stayed because of Cara, she needed me and I needed her.

I turned 10 with no notice from anyone that it was my birthday. It was pure luck that I had found out. I'd found some papers when I was tidying the lounge, they mentioned the house my mother had owned, the fact that it had been sold a long time ago. I wondered what had happened to the money. However, there was my name and my date of birth. No one had celebrated my birthday for years, so it was good to read that day was special. I was good at math, I added up the years I was born and realised I was 10 years old. Wow, double figures already.

That morning I boarded the bus and took my usual seat next to Cara. She didn't greet me with the smile she usually did. Instead her head was turned to the window.

"It's my birthday today, I'm ten," I told her.

When she did turn to me, her eye was black and closed, her lip split. Tears rolled down her cheeks, yet she smiled.

"Happy birthday, Robert," she said.

I just sat and stared, she shook her head gently, a silent ask for me not to talk about it before she turned her face back to the window. I pick up her hand and held it in mine, I didn't care who saw, who sniggered. She was my best friend and I didn't know how to help her.

Cara was quiet for most of the day but at lunchtime we sat together and she shared her lunch with me. After we had eaten she took my hand and we wandered to the prickly plants by the small copse at the back of the school. I now knew those plants to be Aloe Vera and, not that it ever worked, the sticky stuff inside was meant to heal our cuts. Cara turned to me and raised her skirt. Not only were her legs covered in bruises but her white panties were stained red. I stared, open mouthed, not sure if I was to say anything or not. The blood had smeared down her thighs. I watched her body start to shake, she wrapped her arms around herself and for the first time, she cried, really cried. I wanted to hold her, to comfort her, but as I moved towards her she backed away.

"My tummy hurts," she whispered.

"Did he do that?" I asked, my voice cracking on every word.

She didn't answer, she didn't need to. Her lip had started to bleed a little, a small trickle of blood ran down to her chin. As she wiped at it, she smeared it across her face. The tears that were rolling down her cheeks left a clean line through the blood. I was horrified, the sight of her blood stained body stayed with me for many years after.

"I'm going to kill him," I shouted, and I turned and ran.

I heard her calling me, begging me to come back and as I ran Father Peters stepped from the church into my path.

"Where do you think you are going?" He asked.

"Look at her," I screamed. "Look at what he did to her."

"It's not your business, Robert," he said.

"She's my friend and she's hurt."

He reached out and grabbed my arms, I fought, shouting and screaming at him. I was way stronger than he was and I managed to push him away. He stumbled and fell, landing on the dirt path. As I turned to continue my journey I caught sight of Cara, she was bent over, holding her stomach and calling my name. It pulled me up short and I walked back to her. My chest hurt with the anger, my breathing was rapid and I clenched my fists as tight as I could.

"Please, Robert, don't go. He'll kill me if you do. You promised me you wouldn't tell, you promised," she said between her sobs.

"I'm not going anywhere, Cara. Not without you, anyway," I said. "Please, let's run, now. I'll look after you, I won't let anyone hurt you, ever again," I begged.

She just shook her head, resigned to her fate, I guessed. We knelt together on the dusty, dried grass and I held her. By now a crowd had formed, the other kids stood around us. No one spoke and when I looked at them, the hatred must have blazed from my eyes as they backed away. Some time later I heard a man's voice, calling Cara. Before she stood, she placed her hand on my cheek wiping away a tear and then she got up and walked away. I stayed kneeling where I was, crying for the first time ever and finally broken.

****

I never saw Cara again. She didn't get on the bus the following morning, or the one after and I missed her. I walked to where she lived one night, to see if I could find her. There was no sign of her anywhere. She had been the only friend I'd ever had. The only person that had been kind to me, that played with me, that talked to me even. I knew she hadn't moved away, I still saw her parents sometimes, but never Cara. I asked my aunt once, I wanted to know what had happened to her. I don't know why I asked, because I knew, deep down I knew what had happened. I received the worst beating ever that day and was told not to ask questions. I couldn't walk without being hunched over, the scratchy material of my school shirt constantly rubbed at the welts which bled and wept for days. At night I would look up at the stars and wonder if she was looking down at me.

In one way I was envious of Cara, she had escaped her misery, her pain. She was free from it all and I wished I was with her. In my ten year old mind it was better to be dead than alive and beaten.

39546796R00075

Made in the USA
Charleston, SC
15 March 2015